D0007705

HORDE of FOOLS

HORDE of FOOLS

A North-Western Story

James David
Buchanan

Five Star • Waterville, Maine

Five Star First Edition Western Series.

Published in 2001 in conjunction with
Golden West Literary Agency.

Set in 11 pt. Plantin by Minnie B. Raven.

Printed in the United States on permanent paper.

Library of Congress Cataloging-in-Publication Data

Buchanan, James David.
Horde of fools : a north-western story /
James David Buchanan.
p. cm. — (Five Star first edition western series)
ISBN 0-7862-3667-1 (hc : alk. paper)
1. Klondike River Valley (Yukon)—Fiction. 2. Gold mines and mining—Fiction. 3. Women—Alaska—Fiction. 4. Outlaws—Fiction. 5. Alaska—Fiction. I. Title. II. Series.
PS3552.U325 H67 2001
813′.54—dc21 2001040529

"A horde of fools. . . ."

JOHN MUIR

"I've been to college
and smoked cigars. . . ."

CALLIE FISK

Chapter One

Spring came late to New England in the year 1897. At the end of March all of the mountains and some of the hills within view of Bent Creek, Vermont, were still dappled with white. But down in the valley where the road ran straight the first burgeoning signs were all around—hyacinth bulbs sending up scouts, buds on alder and elm, apple orchards on either side showing their first color.

Threatening all of this tranquility, there appeared one Sunday morning a buggy and a carriage and pair racing toward the village, perilously, side by side. The buggy was driven the more recklessly by a lone young woman who had read *Ben-Hur*.

Ahead, Bent Creek Congregational Church was a postcard, a magazine cover, a stereotype, a stereoscopic slide, every white, wooden, spired New England Currier & Ives country church, with horses and buggies tethered outside, ever seen or had existed in peoples' imagination. Covered in snow or framed by leaves and blossoms, it had the power to moisten strong men's eyes on appearance alone.

Right now, it was between seasons and branches were still largely bare, yet the church remained sufficiently beautiful and serene to make the parishioners agonize over how it was they had come to deserve the devotion of Ephraim Fisk. What crime against the Commandments or the Holy Ghost had been, individually or collectively, deliberately or inadvertently, committed in their name?

An earnest but shaky rendition of "Bringing in the

Sheaves" issued forth from the half open doors. Within, the church was packed except for the Fisk pew. Several parishioners, as they sang, let their eyes rove for someone who wasn't there. Even the Reverend Purdy let himself be distracted long enough to glance down at his grandfather's pocket watch.

Out in front again, on the horizon, two small dots and a cloud of dust where the winter mud had dried, all of it advancing toward the church along the main road to town. Tethered horses neighed, sensing an imminent storm. Across the fields and woods came faint clattering and pounding sounds, and shrill voices raised above them. Birds flew out of the trees.

Callie had tied her bonnet to her tightly with a scarf, and a good thing as the wind caused her clothes to stream behind her in a rooster tail. With the lighter equipage and a firm hand on the reins, she was faster and had better control of her one-horse buggy than did her father with the whole rest of the family crowded into his carriage and pair. It was only her tender-heartedness toward her horse, a squeamishness that her father obviously did not share, which impeded her progress.

"You get back to the house, girl!" Ephraim screamed even before he came fully alongside.

"Too late, Papa."

"You're a female, dammit!"

"I know that." Callie couldn't look at her father—it was better to avoid that face on fire—instead concentrated on her driving and the road ahead.

"Then you do what you're told or be damned!"

"Don't curse, Ephraim," his wife Cora begged; it always upset her more on Sundays.

"I'll curse when I damn' please, woman!" he roared with

such force that his beard quivered outwards. "All the horn-toed devils in hell won't see your daughter a prospector in that Sodom."

"I don't care, if I win I'm going," Callie assured him.

"What if you don't, smarty?" her younger sister, Clarissa, yelled over.

"I'll throw myself off Pike's Rock."

"Go ahead, see if anybody catches you," mocked older brother, Homer, a perfect clone of Ephraim, laughing and spitting out the remains of breakfast.

"Oh, shut up, you two."

"Sweetheart, please," Cora cried, taking the suicide threat literally; she was a literal woman.

"I didn't mean it, Mama."

"You want to kill your mother!" Ephraim said, seeing an opening; naturally it was a statement, not a question.

"Ephraim, no," Cora said.

"Mama knows I'm plain and I got no future here."

The church grew larger in their vision, and a few notes of song drifted their way, ignored in the cacophony of their pursuit.

Ephraim roared with increasing desperation: "Sharper than a serpent's tooth an ungrateful daughter!"

"That's 'child.' Ungrateful *child,*" Callie responded.

"You hear that?" the father shouted over his shoulder to his personal choir. "Correctin' her own father? They got a special place in the state prison at Holyoke for girls like that."

Callie spurted ahead to avoid a dangerous narrowing of the road. They were almost at their destination anyway. People inside the church could hear them arrive, hitch the horses, scramble out of the vehicles, and continue an argument that would have blundered through the veil of heaven.

"I just think if you're going to quote Shakespeare you ought to have it right."

"We will come rejoicing . . ."

"That's Scripture, and you'll go up to that Alaska over my dead body."

As she led the way, the whole bunch following behind, Callie got in her last shot: "I wouldn't discount that, Papa."

". . . bringing in the sheaves. . . ."

They trooped up the center aisle to their front row pew, looking neither left nor right, although Callie did manage a quick apologetic smile to the reverend who stood with the Good Book in hand in front of the altar.

"Welcome Brother Ephraim, Cora, young Fisks," he said, smiling down sweetly. "Now we can start church."

"Good idea," the old man responded where no response was expected, "but I ain't your brother."

Callie looked grim while her mother studied the floor. No one gasped or complained, although perhaps there were a few soft sighs. The parishioners had become almost deadened to outrage and were satisfied to let their swift and clever reverend handle it.

"In the brotherhood of Christ, surely. That's all I meant," Purdy stated.

Ripostes like that were one reason Ephraim hated him; he had scarcely sat down and already the slick bastard had him in a box. "Well, maybe that way. . . ."

"Actually, we were waiting for you. Since Miss Callie's requested to be a part of our drawing."

"Don't have nothin' to do with us. She ain't goin'."

"Well, now, Ephraim, the girl's reached her majority and then some, so why don't we just let the Lord settle the question."

"The Lord's a man and a father. He knows which

side his bread's buttered on."

"I knew you'd agree, being the pious soul that you are, so let's get on with it."

Ephraim started to respond but suspected that if he argued the point now he would somehow become "impious." How had that happened? He sat back and tried to figure it out while Callie smiled to herself.

The reverend didn't waste any time. He reviewed how the church was badly in need of funds, as was the whole community, and like many other small towns around America they had hit upon the idea of chipping in to send a native son up to the gold fields. In return for this stake the lucky adventurer would send back the advance and ten percent of their guaranteed fortune.

"Everybody reports the same thing . . . God's bounty lies thick upon the ground for the taking. It only needs a stout heart and a strong back for any enterprising young American."

"I doubt it!" Ephraim called up. "Anyways, get on with your devil's work. We come all this damn' way for a church service."

A couple of bold souls in back shushed him, but the old man ignored them all. Callie flushed and glared. He ignored her, too.

"Plenty of good churches doing it, Brother Fisk, different denominations, all good Christian folk, and they don't consider it the devil's work. First Church of Christ over in Bradyville only last week. 'Course they sent the O'Neil boy, a confirmed idjit. We've got better stock in Bent Creek, I'm sure. . . ."

The Reverend Purdy stepped over to the organ where he claimed a glass bowl full of little slips of paper and brought it to the pulpit.

"Problem is, so many of our fine young men off fighting the perfidious Spaniard." He lowered his head for a moment and murmured: "May the good Lord protect them, each and every one." The congregation joined in a spontaneous: "Amen."

Purdy looked out at his congregation for a moment. The few candidates, all raring to go, stood out like fireflies with their bobbing, twitching white faces against a field of somber church dress. Only Callie's was quiet and tense.

"What we need here is someone who's clever, bold, strong-willed, brave, resourceful. . . ."

Even as he spoke the words, his voice sank away in despair, their hope so obviously in contradiction to the reality confronting him.

"But I expect we also got to be fair about this thing."

Looking out again: bright faces and dim bulbs everywhere, gap-toothed fat boys, peaked mama's boys, the halt and the lame, one with bottle-bottom specs, another a third-grade dropout who couldn't spell gold when asked, a dwarf, a forty-five year old farm hand who had never been out of the county and was suspected of having undue feeling for his mule, twins who were widely recognized as sissies . . . and, of course, one young female.

Outside the big, half open doors the temperature was in the fifties, but the reverend began to sweat. There had been and still was a lot of pressure to disallow Callie because of her sex, not to mention the fact that she was a Fisk. Probably no one disliked her personally; on the contrary, most thought her an excellent schoolteacher for her young age, but it was simply not the sort of task a woman should undertake. In fact, it was downright immoral.

"Now we'll have the drawing." The reverend put his Bible down on the pulpit beside the bowl full of names and looked to the congregation, holding his hands behind his back. Silently, to himself, he said: *Forgive me, O Lord.*

The only person present who could see behind his back was the hair-bunned organist, a maiden lady of sixty-five with the complexion of a dried tomato. Her life had been bad, but her sense of humor was good. It came into play now by virtue of the fact that absolutely nothing showed on her face, although she could clearly see with what clumsiness the reverend moved a slip of paper, fixed on his wrist with stickum, to his palm. Fortunately in its new location he did a better job of concealment.

"Let us bow our heads and pray. Lord, bless this decision with Your divine wisdom. And try not to judge too harshly those who, out of ignorance or just plain orneriness, dispute Your holy word in this."

The congregation joined him in a particularly enthusiastic "Amen," which was then punctuated by Ephraim's loud—"Buncha bunk!"—as he waved it off in spectacular fashion.

The reverend finally reached in to stir for dear life. Now the crucial paper was stuck to his palm, and, while he struggled to get it between his fingers, he had to keep stirring . . . and stirring . . . and. . . .

"Gold rush's gonna be over, Reverend!" one of the parishioners called good-naturedly to general laughter.

"So's this town," someone else said with less cheer.

Finally Purdy got control of the slip; he was never cognizant of the organist's deep exhalation. He withdrew his hand with a little flourish, wafted it back and forth as if that would validate it, opened it up, and read: "The blessed pilgrim, according to God's will, is . . . Miss Callie Fisk!"

Amidst a stunned silence, Callie was the first to react, jumping to her feet with a squeal and then up and down, crying: "Oh! Oh! Oh!" Delphi Fisk squealed, too, and Cora murmured a fervent: "Thank you, Lord." Ephraim and the other children seemed pole axed. A couple of the losers groaned or commented unhappily.

Callie committed an unknowing gaff in running up and hugging and thanking the reverend, to which he replied nervously: "The *Lord* chose you, dear, not me." And: "He works in mysterious ways his wonders. . . ."

Just as a couple of the women uttered—"Bless you."—a couple of men began to complain loudly. The reaction could have gone either way. Then Ephraim's bull voice took over: "I forbid it! No female daughter of mine's. . . ."

Purdy tried to regain control by speaking rapidly and raising his voice above the old man's. "God go with you, my child, in this divine quest. . . ." He broke it off when that sounded hyperbolic even to him. "When can you leave?"

". . . goin' up there with that preverted buncha idlers and outlaws, that pesthole of sin and corruption. Not even this one!"

"I have my suitcase in the buggy," Callie responded.

The reverend experienced a certain tightening of the sphincter as Callie's father advanced, brandishing an upraised fist.

"You can stay with us tonight," the reverend said, shaking but brave.

The organist realized something must be done to prevent a riot and, starting off the singing herself at the top of her frail old lungs, she burst into "The Battle Hymn of the Republic."

"Mine eyes have seen the glory of the coming of the Lord. . . ."

"You better unpack, missy, 'fore I whup you black and blue!"

Cora and Delphi could still be heard crying, so the organist sang even louder, waving encouragement to the congregation. A song to rouse the dead, it did, and gradually everyone joined in if only to try and drown out Ephraim's blasphemies.

"He is trampling out the vintage where the grapes of wrath are stored. . . ."

"Not any more, Papa. I'm stronger than you, and I have an iron will."

He hesitated to hit her—and lost the war on the spot. "Damn your eyes . . ."

"He has loosed the fateful lightning of his terrible swift sword. . . ."

". . . you devil's bitch, you whore of Babylon!"

There were wails of despair at this new level of sacrilege from some of the women, unprecedented within these pure white walls. Some put fingers in their ears or covered those of their children who otherwise would have had a decent chance to enjoy this little contretemps.

The reverend's voice soared: "Lord, forgive our wayward brother his intemperance and loud voice. His heart is clouded with hate, Lord, and he knoweth not what he is at."

Callie, triumphant for the first time in her life, stood before the whole congregation and sang as loudly as anyone. "In the valley of the lilies, Christ was born across the sea. . . ."

Ephraim turned to his family and shouted louder than anyone could possibly sing: "On your feet, daughters! Your sister's goin' to hell, and we're goin' to the Baptists!"

He stomped out, leading the train, as the music and singing swelled in a futile attempt to drown their passing.

"With the glory in his bosom that transfigured you and me. . . ."

* * * * *

That night Callie cut off her glorious long hair and cried a lot. She figured it would be the last time she could afford to.

Chapter Two

In the Territory of Alaska spring always came late and winter early, like some men's luck. The man in a blue parka who was lying on his back atop a small hill, reading, believed in making his own luck. He had been successful at it, too. At least, he was known throughout the territory.

Warm and chilly were relative terms away from the glaciers, but he had adapted well to the climate and showed no signs of discomfort on this cool, cloudy morning. Did he even need the parka; it was more of a talisman and a signature. The hill upon which he waited was showing signs of hope, the grass was halfway to green, and the scrub was showing a few buds. His best season was coming.

Claude Emmett was not symmetrical and winning in his parts, but he was tall and possessed a certain jauntincss of style and manner, eyes that danced the mazurka in the presence of a pretty female, and an original turn of mind that made people, especially women, think he was damned handsome. Men reacted to his rough face, rough wit, sense of competence and yet dash. Everyone likes a mystery.

A certain soiled dove who knew him only too well once told him he had two sets of eyes, one for civilization and one for his chosen profession; she had seen both and wished she hadn't.

Gradually distant voices, even their whispers bouncing off the walls of the hills and cliffs lining the valley, insinuated their way into his distraction. Slowly he closed the book and stood.

Climbing to the cusp of the hill he could hear someone whistling "Casey Would Waltz with the Strawberry Blonde." Peering over, four men were herding mules up the rugged trail below and straight toward him. They were a bit closer than he had realized. Didn't matter, he was ready.

Three of the approaching party were older with hard, sharp, jaded urban faces, while the fourth was a more rural sweeter-looking youngster. At this remove it was possible to make out the roulette wheels, dice cages, and other gambling paraphernalia strapped on the mules.

All of them, even the kid who was the whistler, seemed chilled, unaccustomed to the harsh climate, huddled into their parkas. The lips of one of the older men moved as if he was swearing continuously under his breath, but there was no conversation now, a sure sign that they were feeling miserable. Cheechakos could never easily bear the huge, wanton emptiness beyond the towns—that took time and grit.

Claude didn't have to see them further; he rested with his back to a boulder and listened to the clackings, snortings, bangings, and whistling. When they sounded close enough to step on him, he tied a bandanna across his face, stood, and stepped out onto the trail.

"Hold on there, boys." He had a deep resonant voice that served him in his occupation by carrying well on the cold air. But then, what was a voice without leveled pistols?

The men bunched up on a trail that was too narrow for a fast turnaround. The few seconds necessary to throw off their lethargy and surprise evolved into a tableau of gaping faces. Claude was prepared to wait through that.

"Shit!" the first gambler managed finally.

"Don't do anything foolish. I'll shoot your damn' eyes right out your bungholes."

Had they been clever and alert they might have hoped to report back—assuming they lived—on the bandit's observable characteristics, the obvious ones of height, weight, coloring, but more to the point that, although his language was rough, his speech indicated an education. Claude, however, seldom robbed anyone perspicacious. That was another way he was smart.

The second gambler in line leaned out to look past his buddy and exclaimed: "Great God Almighty . . . it's the Blue Parka Man!"

"Seems I am. Throw your pokes on the ground with your pistols."

The first gambler turned to the others: "Don't fool with him, don't dare."

"Good advice."

They began, with some under-the-breath grumbling, to untie the small sacks of nuggets or dust at their waists or drag them out of their saddlebags to be dropped where they were.

"I watched you gentlemen capture half the gold in Klondike City the other night. Matter of fact, some of it was mine."

"Which was you?" the first gambler asked.

"The one wasn't worried."

"Blackjack or monte?"

"You just keep handing it over."

The first was the slick, obviously. "Seeing, sir, as you and we are, in a manner of speaking, in the same line of work. . . ."

Claude wagged the long barrel of a Navy Colt at him. "Horse shit. I don't cheat, I steal honest, right out in God's sunshine. There's no comparing."

Thinking that he might be distracted by this ethical debate, the third gambler, who by the looks of him might have been the muscle but certainly not the brains, tried to take advantage by slipping a small pistol out of the inside of his parka.

"That's a bit to the philosophical side for me, sir," the slick said, "but I have to take your. . . ."

Claude detected the close-to-the-vest movement behind this one and jumped aside for a clearer view even as he fired the Colt. The big man let out a cry of shock and pain as the bullet tore off his ear. Something besides cartilage, too, was struck because blood mushroomed and flowed down his cheek to form an underground river beneath his shirt. As his hand whipped up to the ear, the pistol flew out of it. All four mules spooked, rearing up and hawing, and for a few moments there was chaos with everyone except Claude shouting something contradictory.

He waited tensely, eyes lit up and half crouched, ready to fire again and shoot all four if necessary.

The second gambler shouted at his reckless comrade: "You damned fool, you see how he shoots?"

"I was aiming for his forehead," Claude stated.

"He's kilt me, anyways. I'm bleedin' to death."

"Aw, shut up," the second gambler told him, as he started making a bandage.

"Now you got any more gold, jewels, or money, you just shake it loose. I'm not foolin'. Better get some whisky on that, too." He indicated the third gambler.

This encouraged everyone to dig further into their clothing. While this was going on, the youngest managed to ease his way through the others to confront Claude, wearing a hangdog expression on his callow face.

"Sir, I've heard about you. We all have over in Tamish Valley . . . Robin Hood of the North."

"Well, that part's a mite exaggerated. You got any gold there . . . cough it up, boy."

"What I wanted to say, sir, I'm not with these men. I just went along for protection."

"Poor choice."

"See, I got to git me back to my wife. She's in a family way over in our valley. Please, sir, we don't have 'nuff bacon an' beans to hardly git through the month. That's why I come over to Klondike City to find work. I been cleanin' spittoons an'. . . ."

"All right, boy. I don't want to hear all that. You go on." Claude reached into his own pocket to pull out a gold nugget, and flipped it to the surprised kid. "Git!"

The young man's face lit like a stage. "Whoooeeee! God bless you, mister." He started backing away. "I'm gonna tell ever'body back home how I met the Blue Parka Man and he really is a Robin Hood. . . ." He ran back down the trail, but paused to shout back: "If I knew your name, we'd call our young 'un after you!"

Claude didn't bother to shout; it wasn't like the kid needed the information. "That's an honor I'll have to forego." Anyway, by now the kid had almost disappeared out of sight around a bend.

The leader started to laugh, a sound like a seal celebrating.

"What the hell you laughin' at, you ugly bastard?" Claude asked.

"You just got soaped, my friend. That there was a real honest-to-God confidence trickster, name of Kid Jimmy Fresh. An' you give him your gold!"

The second gambler overheard, abandoned his patient, and joined in the hilarity. "Lord-a-God, he flimflammed the Blue Parka Man. That's somethin' to take outta all this."

Claude looked in the direction of the absent kid and shook his head. "Well, it's on his conscience. I don't mind telling you, I could do a lot better in this profession if I was willing to lower my standards. Now git yourselves!" He fired his gun in the air and, feeling a little scratchier than he wanted to admit, kicked at them as they turned their mules and trundled back the way they had come.

The wounded gambler was still whining, but he went along as swiftly as the other two, shouting after them: "I'm bleedin' to death. Help me!"

Claude yelled—"You want me to make 'em even?"—and fired another shot past his head, spurring him on. Even the mules were flying and flopping by now.

When he finally got around to collecting his loot, his mood considerably improved. The small hole in the mountains he maintained as his bank would be receiving a goodly deposit. He just hoped the horse could handle it so he wouldn't have to walk.

Down in the center of the valley, a figure leading an ancient swayback nag struggled along a different trail traversing the flat. Seen at a mile, anyone could have marked the fatigue and the fact that the traveler was wearing a nondescript city jacket unsuited to the north and pants that were a couple of sizes too large. Closer, they would have been surprised to find that it was a young woman whose clothes and well-being were even less than they had appeared. She also wore a man's battered, snap-brimmed hat tied to her head with earmuffs beneath it.

The horse's hoofs dragged, but it would have been hard to say if that was more pronounced than Callie's stumbling walk. She was thinner than the healthy farm girl who had left Bent Creek fixed on conquest: sunburned and chilled, her lips parched and cracked, fatigue and discouragement showing in smudges around the eyes and mouth.

She paused to consult a pocket compass and, in looking up at the sky for a check, spotted the three gamblers and their mules racing down out of the hills, indifferent to trails or anything else.

She waved both hands and shouted as loudly as she could: "Hey, there! Halloooo! Help! I need. . . ."

There was no hope of their paths intersecting and very little that the men would have stopped if they had.

Callie sought shelter by a row of boulders and a single tree on that largely treeless landscape, to which she tied the horse. Having broken a few branches off the tree, she was trying to start a fire with a flint. Eventually she produced a little smoke, blown upon mightily to provide a brief flare-up, but then the mostly green wood would refuse to hold on to the fire and it would fade.

She got it to smolder finally, so let it go at that and sat with her back against the tree, watching the smoke slowly waft away. Digging deeply into her coat pocket, she came up with a piece of hardtack and part of a brown apple. When the horse was seen looking longingly at her, she got up to give him half of what remained and almost lost her hand. She flopped down again, exhausted and discouraged.

Until. . . . She was not alone. There was someone else out there on the flat. Someone coming in her direction mounted on . . . it could have been a horse or a mule. She watched for a long time, the figure—difficult to make out whether it was male or female because the sun had come out behind it. Male would have been a good guess in this God-and-woman-forsaken land. Unless it was her imagination. It seemed to be coming faster and faster. It was definitely a mule. She squinted and shaded her eyes.

The figure seemed to be white from head to toe, dirty white, but his constant bouncing up and down made it difficult to make out why. Gradually a beard could be seen along with a lot of flowing salt and pepper hair and a fixed expression, or at least the way he held his head up suggested that. There was a relentlessness to the way he kept coming on . . . closer. . . .

Callie's first reaction had been one of relief, even of joy, but that was followed by a slowly dawning sense of the bizarre nature of the apparition. The man was wearing nothing but long johns and didn't have a saddle. He didn't have an expression, either. Blank. Faster and faster, straight at her. Actually whipping the poor beast into a rapid trot now. She called—"Hello!"—but there was no response.

For a fatal few moments she was locked in place by fear and simple fascination. He had been a large man but was hollowed out by hunger and cold. In fact, his skin looked blue, and so it should, dressed, or undressed, like that. He was still as rigid as an ice sculpture, and his eyes were so empty of feeling he could have been dead. And yet she knew that he was alive.

Callie rushed to the horse, tripped on her too-long pants, fell, scrambled to her feet, and then fought to get an elderly double-barreled shotgun out of its improvised rope holster on the saddle. One of the finger pulls on the hammers caught, and her panicky movements attempting to get it loose spooked the horse. Old and tired as it was, it kicked, spun, and snorted like a captive stallion, tossing its head violently from side to side. It was all Callie could do to hang on for her life.

"Whoa! Hold! Hold! Stop it, horse! Lord, have mercy. . . ."

The daunting figure was almost upon her. She could

hear his fevered panting and smell him above the odor even of her own horse. His bloodshot eyes seemed to fill her whole horizon. Finally she calmed the nag enough to be able to yank loose the shotgun. It was heavy, and she had never fired it, so getting it cocked and pointed took up more crucial seconds.

Those seconds were the difference between life or death, which would have surprised no one in this harsh land. The specter whipped the beast right up to her and dove off. He missed his target but reached out to catch her neck with his forearm as he went by.

Callie managed to fire one barrel, but unfortunately it was at the planets as she went tumbling. Hitting the ground, hard, made the weapon fly out of her hands and clatter along the still half-frozen ground. She managed a partial scream before the wind was knocked out of her, and afterwards it was necessary to use all she had in the fight.

The man jumped on top of her, trying to sit astride but being bucked in every direction. He was still able to begin tearing off items of clothing. Callie being layered for warmth with bits and pieces, however, made it confusing as well as difficult, especially while she continued to fight. Reaching up to punch him in the face only got her slapped twice as hard in return.

His face again became her whole sky, red eyes set in bluish-green skin, tangled hair and beard, blackened stumps of teeth, and septic breath his terror weapons. And yet he never said a word, which made it worse—was he human? Callie again tried to scream.

While she didn't know everything, she had grown up on a farm and had some idea of the horror to which she could be subjected by a creature as loathsome as this. Death was secondary.

When she managed to dislodge him for a moment, he merely grabbed one of her boots and started dragging her around on the ground in an attempt to free it. At one point she was pulled through the pathetic remains of her attempt to build a fire and, since she was burned only slightly, had reason to celebrate her own ineptitude. There was no doubt that this was someone who would push her face into burning embers to get what he wanted.

It wasn't long before Callie was down to her bloomers and half of a man's shirt, and they were giving way even though she held on grimly. The assailant, still on top, was slapping her into submission. Battered and sobbing, she continued to struggle and managed to bite his hand. He gave a primeval cry, his first sound above a grunt, and hit her on the side of the face with his fist. For a moment she was in danger of going under.

The shot, a loud crack, struck a rock a few feet away from the struggle like a lightning bolt, splitting it. Sparks and chips also went flying, one stinging Callie. The man on top of her froze for a second, then leaped off and spun in circles, looking for the source of this new threat, his eyes swelling hugely with alarm, like twin Arctic suns.

Callie scooted away, at the same time trying frantically to gather up enough clothes to cover herself. Because now there was someone else on the scene, an altogether different but not necessarily reassuring man. Up on a small rise above them, an outlined figure in a blue parka, a bandanna over his face, and a pointed Remington. At that angle he was terrifying, or there was something terrifying about him—his ungodly calm in this situation.

"The lady declines," Claude said. He blew out the smoke and brought the gun to bear again. Callie's attacker seemed to hear him, but he dove for the shotgun anyway.

"Don't!" Claude yelled. The madman ignored that, too, standing and trying to get the gun pointed. "Damn' fool!" Claude shot him through the heart. "Aw, shit!"

The man turned away, pitched forward, and rolled, blood spreading through the front of his greasy gray underwear. If he made a sound, it was an expiration, and it would have been drowned out by Callie's healthy scream anyway.

Claude stomped down from the hillock, communicating his unhappiness with his walk. At the approach of the opposite sex, Callie stopped screaming long enough to scramble for the rest of her clothes.

"Look what you made me do," Claude complained.

Holding some of her rags in front of her, Callie approached the body from one side, while her rescuer came from the other. "Is he dead?"

"Mortally." He nudged the body with his foot.

"*You* shot him. You killed this man!" She knew that she sounded a little hysterical and regretted it, but then she had never seen a man shot. "I didn't want that."

"Fooled me."

"Don't you patronize me!" She heard her voice growing stronger. Maybe it was a good thing to get mad at someone after all that she had suffered during the past weeks. "I could have stopped him. He'd never've had his way with me."

The stranger chuckled. "You think that's what he was after?"

Callie didn't know what to say; not only was she confused but the whole topic was so distasteful. "Wha . . . what do you mean?" Immediately she regretted asking.

"He didn't want you . . . he couldn't've raised the flag if his life depended on it . . . he wanted your clothes." He turned the corpse over with his boot. "Look at him." Callie averted her face and shuddered. "Been blue-ticketed to the coast."

"What's that mean?" She backed away and tried to seem indifferent.

"God and Mister Remington gave you back your finery. Maybe you better put 'em on."

"It's all torn. Turn your back."

Claude thought it was silly, but he complied. "Miners' court. He must've broke into somebody's food cache up in the fields. This is the ticket they give you out of there, a mule and your underwear."

"Why blue?"

"That's what you are when they find you."

"Oh, that's terrible."

"That's justice."

"You still turned around?"

"You'll have to trust me."

"Why do you have that scarf across your face?"

"I'm cold."

"You're a road agent."

"I'm an entrepreneur. I'm reorganizing the economy of this place. You talk too damn' much."

"And you swear too much. But I'm used to that. My papa cusses more than anybody in Vermont. Mama says. . . ."

"Are you finished? 'Cause. . . ."

Callie had restored her clothes to the proper places, although there were a few gaps that weren't there before and some pieces hanging loose. "You can look now."

Claude turned. "I'd like to tell you it was an improvement, but even I won't lie that much."

Callie bristled. "I'm decent, aren't I? I don't know where

you come from, but back in Vermont that's what counts most."

"Glad I never been there. Why'd you cut off your hair?"

"I'm not interested in putting on the dog for a bunch of lascivious men. I'm here on a serious errand. I'm a sourdough."

She said it with such earnestness, Claude couldn't stop himself from laughing. "You a sourdough?" He laughed harder. "Yes, you are, young lady, a real honest-to-God sourdough. I can see that."

"Who are you to laugh at me? At least, sir, I make my living through hard work."

"That's probably why you look like that." He was finding himself terribly amusing.

"I look like this because everything I had was stolen in Skagway. Good Christian people at the Salvation Army gave me these things, such as they are."

"You got through there with your skin you're lucky." Bringing himself under control, Claude asked: "You got a shovel? I want to get this wahoo planted 'fore the wolves get him." He poked around for some soft ground.

"Wolves?"

"You think you were at the Chicago Exposition? Wolves are some of the nicer people we got." He stopped and studied her. "You got chilled. That's not a thing you want to let happen."

Callie was still so full of adrenalin she had to feel her own body with her hands to realize that it was probably true. It made her shiver.

"I'm camped just over there. Better get some hot java in you and a fire 'fore you go back on trail. I probably got a needle and thread and a spare blanket." She hesitated. "I'll take care of him later."

"I don't have a shovel. I was going to buy one."

"I'll put rocks over him. Come on."

"You don't even like me."

"It's a hard country. We take care of each other up here." He turned away.

"Wait." She went over and picked up the shotgun. "It's not that I don't trust you. It's the wolves."

Shaking his head, Claude started back the way he had come. She could follow or not.

Chapter Three

"Damn! Dammit all to hell!"

"There you go again," Callie sighed.

"That hurt!" He used the tail of his scarf to wipe steaming coffee from his chin. "How you expect me to get something hot under this thing without my burning myself? If you weren't so god-damned distrustful."

"Oh, stop grousing. Here, put it on me if you must." She turned away, and Claude moved over behind to take off the scarf and refit it over her eyes. "I think you're being silly. Maybe you ought to get a proper mask if you're going to keep on doing this."

"What do you know about it? I saved your damn' hide . . . doesn't that count for anything?" Freed, he lit up the stub of a cigar.

Callie had to think. "I suppose, but you were awfully rude. And it's only what a gentleman should do."

"You put a lot of store in manners. Besides, I'm not a gentleman, I'm a road agent, remember? Want more of this mud?"

She held out her cup for him to fill it and tried to brighten. "Would you shoot me if I saw your face?"

"Uhn-huh."

"I've always been one to test things out, Papa says. . . ."

"Go home, what's-your-name."

"I can't. Callie Fisk. What's yours?"

"Look here, you're a girl."

"That's why I can't. Anyhow, I've come all the way from

Bent Creek, Vermont, and I'm not someone to be turned back when people have put their trust in me. I have an iron will, and I'm going on to Daughton, and that's it."

He looked quizzical; some alarm had been sounded but as yet it was indistinguishable. "Where?"

"Daughton."

"Aaaaah, Dogtown!" He repeated it to himself, as if hearing of a lost continent. "For such a little girl you sure can find big trouble."

"I'm not a little girl" she said indignantly. "I'm five foot six and a half and a woman, and I don't like to be addressed in that manner, thank you." She also seemed to feel a need to explain: "Food's expensive up here. I've lost a lot of weight. Besides, what's wrong with this . . . Dogtown, as you call it?"

"It'd take too long to tell."

"The gold's in Daughton."

"So's hell."

She stood, setting her jaw. "If you'd be so kind as to point me in the right direction. Without robbing me or anything."

"What'd be the point of it?" He rose, also, brushed at his pants, and pointed off to the northeast. "You go along that trail . . . you might want to take off the blindfold!"

"Oh." She started to reach up for it.

He snarled—"Turn around, first!"—so loudly, Callie jumped.

"You don't have to shout at me." She turned away in a huff to snatch off the blindfold and throw it back over her shoulder. "Why should I care who you are? I thought men like you were supposed to be bold and dashing, weren't afraid of anything."

"I can see where you haven't known a whole lot of trail

robbers." He took the scarf and tied it across his face, muffling his words somewhat. "You not only talk too much, you read too much." He knelt and dug around in his pack.

"I'm not interested in your opinion."

"Here, the blanket, you better take it." He tried to hand it to her.

"No, thank you."

"At least take it for the horse." He offered again, and this time, after some drawing back, she reluctantly accepted.

"Better take some jerky to be safe . . . you're already too skinny for up here. Woman needs some meat on her."

She stamped her foot. "I hate being indebted to a man of your kind."

"You'll starve."

"I'd rather."

"Yeah, I can see you haven't tried that, either. Look here, I told you, it's a hard country. This is so you'll share with the next fool you meet on the trail who's got himself in a fix."

"I hadn't thought of it that way." She looked at him with genuine curiosity for the first time. "Even bandits care about such things up here?"

"Come on." He took her hand and pulled her atop a boulder. Turning her shoulders so she would face the east, he pointed again. "That way . . . till you get to Border Creek, then follow it north. This is important . . . be sure and stay on this side of it. Whatever you do, don't cross over. That's Canada and the Mountie up there shoots trespassers on sight."

She looked at him to see if he was teasing but, from what she could see of his face, he seemed perfectly serious. "That can't be. A policeman would never do that?" Her shocked tone suggested she already believed, at least in part, that it was possible.

"This one would." He reached up to help her down. She took it but jumped away from him. She was learning.

"Good grief, everyone's mad."

"Just about. One thing. . . ." He put his hand on her shoulder.

She flinched slightly but recovered and looked embarrassed. An extra effort was required to meet his eyes above the scarf. No one in Bent Creek had eyes like that, which seemed to be always surveying an unknown ground for any sign of life so they could swoop down and put an end to it. When you were close to him, you felt hot. It was scary. And a little exciting.

"Yes?" She had allowed the hand to remain. It began to raise goose bumps under all those layers of raggedy clothes.

"I'd appreciate it . . . that is, if you feel you owe me anything . . . your forgetting about how you saw me out here, my shooting that fella and all. There's enough enthusiasm for seeing me dangle as it is."

When she didn't respond, too busy with her own thoughts, he appeared to be rethinking it. "The only way I could count on that, I suppose, is to kill you. Oh, hell, that'd be a waste after I went and saved you. No, I think I'll put you on your honor. I can tell you got a lot of that. More than most sane people."

"I do. But on the other hand, you are a wanted criminal and. . . ."

A man who had never put up his hands for anyone threw them in the air in frustration. "Aw, for God's sake, Miss Fisk!"

Callie would hate herself later for sounding like a schoolteacher, but when she was indignant, it just flowed, unstoppable as lava. "I was just going to say yes, and thank you, but as usual your impossible rudeness intervened to spoil it. I won't betray you. There, I said it. I thank you."

"You won't after you seen Dogtown."

Sergeant Clarence McDonald was a straight-arrow officer, spit and polish, except for the single oddity of shooting on sight anyone who crossed the border into Canada. In extreme situations, where he recognized the miscreant for an undesirable, he had been known to fire at them while they were still thinking about it.

On a cool, clear afternoon he lay in the shrubbery atop a hill overlooking a creek, one tiny segment of what constituted his patrol area stretching across hundreds of square miles of wilderness. The creek didn't have an official name, or it had dozens, depending on who had passed by lately or who was spinning the tale. On the local maps it was simply designated "border creek" without capitals.

Mac stroked his mustache and studied the two men approaching across the enormous meadow that marked the other side of the creek. He removed his fur hat, afraid that it might stand too high and be seen, and tried sighting along his standard issue single-shot Lee-Enfield rifle. He flopped onto his back to wait, studying the clouds. After a while, he rolled onto his stomach again, rubbed his eyes vigorously to clear them, and lined up his shot.

Just below, there was a little cobbled-together wooden bridge across the creek. The two men were poised to cross it if they ever stopped arguing. They stood holding the reins of their horses, arms waving and heads bobbing. Their voices carried up to him on the crisp spring air, but, while the intent was clear enough, the individual words were lost. It didn't matter; they would cross or they wouldn't.

The youngest of the two hulks was Jorem Swope, in his early twenties. His small eyes in a small head on such a large body along with a malevolent squint gave him the unpleasant aspect of a big snapping turtle. To somewhat balance those lines, he generally wore a Western-style hat—many of the Swopes did—and a mustache that drooped at both ends. His hope had been that it would become shaggy in the cowboy tradition, but, while it was sufficiently unkempt, filled out as it was with the remains of porridge, eggs, and burnt beans, it remained doggedly thin and straggled, exhausted, to the finish line of his jowls. He wore a weathered calfskin jacket that made him look pale, highlighting his acne, and snakeskin boots with spurs.

The older man, King Otto, about forty, was more of a fit with the land, skin burned by sun off the snow and beaten into jerky by the wind. Hair and beard were wiry, thick; individual hairs grew everywhere out of his face and neck, in his view a practical necessity. One lower and two upper front teeth were missing with the rest on the way, giving him a perpetual scowl of pain. He wore a fur cap, long coat, and trail boots.

Both men had rifles on the horses and a pistol on one hip, Jorem's pearl-handled.

"He could be up there right now," King Otto argued. "Watchin' us. How would we know?"

"He cain't be ever'where at once't. There's over a hunnert miles for him to watch over. He ain't no demon."

"There's some say he is. I changed my mind. I ain't goin'."

"And what about that miners' posse? You think they ain't still back of us? They don't give up."

"Don't be a damn' fool. They ain't never seen our faces.

We could go to Klondike City. Anywheres but Dogtown for me."

Atop the hill, Mac, still having trouble adjusting his aim, finally slipped a pair of wire-rimmed spectacles onto the bridge of his nose. When he looked down the sights again, it was with a sigh of pleasure.

"We're goin' to Dawson," Jorem screamed, "an' god damn you for a yeller Chinaman!" He yanked out his pearl-handle and jammed it into the other's midsection just above the belt. He was proud of his speed, having practiced it in front of many a mirror in imitation of accounts in dime novels.

"Don't you call me yellow, you little snot-nosed. . . ."

"You shut your mouth, King!" Jorem yelled, so loud Mac could make out every word. "I'll call you anything I damn' please, long as you can feel this in your belly, and you won't call me nothin'! You hear? It's safer in Canada, and the poon's younger and sweeter than those ol' pox-pumpers we got in Dogtown. 'Sides, I'm more afraid of Daddy than I am of you or some damn' redcoat."

King Otto had cooled a bit and looked down at the long barrel disappearing a half inch into his bulge. "I guess you're right. Mountie can't be every damn' where at once." He nodded and stepped away and, when Jorem didn't shoot him, took that as permission to mount his horse. He wanted to get across while his nerve was up.

Jorem put the gun away and mounted his own. King Otto drew his pistol, let out a whooping war cry, and dug in his heels. The startled horse balked, then leaped ahead. Within a couple of those long strides they were clattering across the bridge.

Jorem had pretended to be on his way to doing the same thing, but now hung back an instant to watch.

Otto was almost across when the *bang* of a rifle echoed through the trees on the hills above, and he pitched backward, blood on his shirtfront, pulling his horse's head back with him until he tumbled out of the saddle. His heavy body, striking the bridge, almost broke through its rotting timbers.

The horse nearly went down, too, but struggled as only a poor dumb beast can when terrified by the unknown. All four legs seemed to fly in different directions, the huge eyes rolled in a tossing head until finally it righted itself and scrambled full around. One hoof slipped off the edge in the desperate fight for purchase, then it leaped over its fallen rider and fled back into the United States, less from any motives of patriotism than the fact that it was now pointed in that direction.

Jorem, who had been entering the bridge when his partner was shot, whipped his own horse around, and sped off inland a full quarter mile.

Up on the ridge line, Mac patted his rifle and smiled. Complacency was short-lived; the next time he looked it was with a different emotion. Frowning, he removed his glasses and wiped them quickly. There it was, what he had thought he had seen but had trouble believing—King Otto was up on his feet, running, stumbling back onto American soil. Son-of-a-bitch had lead in his pencil, you had to give him that.

Mac tried to line up a hasty shot, but it posed a conundrum; he had no problem with shooting them on American soil if, for instance, they were shooting back. After all, who was to see or give witness except some lout who was going to be hung on sight anyway? But to shoot a running man, a wounded man, in the back, that was another thing. He had already done his duty in foiling an attempt at illegal entry.

On the other hand, he knew that creature down there to be the sort who would kill an old lady or small child or whole bunches of both for a dime on the dollar. How many of those was he dooming to death by failing to pull the trigger? This question weighed heavily. Sometimes it was tough being Presbyterian.

By the time it was settled in his mind, King Otto was hiding behind a large alluvial boulder down on the plain and throwing wild pistol shots in Mac's direction. Fortunately his rifle had been carried off by the bolting horse. There was no danger of the Mountie being hit, but now he was stuck here, obligated to do something. You didn't leave a dog to die in this country.

Mac put down the rifle to think it over and have a sip of tea from his canteen—that was another mistake. Next time he looked, here came the other one riding back fast and loose to join his companion. When Jorem got to the boulder, he leaped down and rolled behind it before Mac, frantically grabbing up his weapon, could get him in his sights.

King Otto was even more surprised to find that his partner had returned for him—after all, he knew him. Jorem slid up close, so that both were sitting with their backs to the rock. Mac rang a shot off the top of it that made a nasty noise and sent dust into the air. Both ducked instinctively.

It caused Otto to clutch his stomach, which seemed to be pumping out blood at an alarming rate, with one hand while his gun hand lay slack on the ground, the pistol itself loose in his fingers. He was paling rapidly and breath came in fits and starts with unpleasant gurgling sounds between. It took a few seconds to gather enough breath for speech.

"You come back for me. You didn't leave me."

Jorem's answer was to reach over and begin tugging at his partner's belt.

"What're you doin'?"

"Gimme your damn' poke."

"What?"

"The gold we stole, your half." He yanked the little bag free. "Don't be selfish, you ain't gonna need it."

"You damn' little pinhead . . . ," he broke off, coughing and spitting blood. "That's why you come. . . ."

" 'Course it is," Jorem said matter-of-factly, taking off his hat as he stretched up to look over the top of the boulder, then was driven back by a shot that rained dust and chips on his hair. "God damn he can shoot, that one. I'll git him someday sure for this."

Otto tried to pick up his pistol, but it fell through his fingers. "You son-of-a-bitch! You damn' weasel . . . gimme back. . . ."

Jorem ignored him, checked his gun, put his hat back on, and crouched. "You're jist jealous 'cause you're dyin' and I ain't." He jumped up, fired off three shots in the general direction of Mac's position, and ran, zigzagging, for his horse where it grazed a few yards away.

King Otto yelled after him: "You burn in hell, Jorem Swope!"

Demonstrating surprising skill, Jorem managed to keep the beast between Mac and himself, running alongside of it until he could heave himself up into the saddle. Hunched over, keeping his own head behind that of the horse's, he fled across the valley, again following an evasive course.

Mac fired two shots after him, missed, sighted again . . . but stopped himself. Perplexed, he slowly lowered the rifle.

It was necessary to use binoculars to identify the oncoming Callie, pushing her old bag of bones for all he was worth, legs sticking out, one hand on her head to keep her hat from flying off, everything in danger of flying off, including Callie. She went right by Jorem, but, bent on escape, he failed even to look at her.

Mac couldn't figure it out. Was this creature—he couldn't tell if it was male or female but naturally assumed the former since almost everyone was—bent on rescue, self-destruction, illegal immigration, or just a plain lunatic.

King Otto saw her coming and shrieked: "Help! Help me!"

She rode up to him and dismounted, indifferent to her own safety.

"Get down! He'll shoot!"

Callie went to him and knelt. "Who? What's happened here?"

"You blind, kid?! I'm gut shot. That crazy Mountie done it. No . . . warnin'. . . ." He began to cough and gasp again.

"Here, let me look."

"I don't need you lookin'. Get me to a sawbones, for Christ's sake."

"You needn't curse. Here, let me look. . . ."

She pulled open his coat and shirt, revealing a hairy, blood soaked belly that heaved unnaturally. She reached under her own clothes and tore off a piece of shirt tail, folded it neatly, applied it to the wound, and pressed it there. "I never had anything to do with a man's stomach before, but I believe I can help."

While she worked, Otto squinted at her as if examining someone hopelessly insane. "Say, you're a young girl."

"You have any whisky?"

"You're not gettin' it!" Even critically wounded, he managed to screw his face into something pugnacious.

"I don't drink and I don't have any tincture of iodine . . .

I need it for an antiseptic. I'm trying to save your life."

"Oh. I was gonna die drunk if nobody come."

He pulled a flask out of his coat pocket and handed it over. Callie poured it on the makeshift bandage, bringing a howl of pain from Otto that rang through the hills like a moose call.

"Good grief. Back home women in labor don't make that big a ruckus. Hold that there and let me get something." She went out to her horse.

"You there! Hello."

She turned and looked across the creek and up at the hill. Mac was standing silhouetted in an unintentionally heroic posture. He had taken off the spectacles, not that Callie could see it from where she was.

Unconcerned, she dug through her saddlebag while yelling back: "Did you do this?"

"You're a woman."

"I know. People keep telling me." She found what she wanted and went back to her patient.

"Stay away from him. He's a bad one."

She told Otto: "Here, I had a plaster in my kit." She applied it to his stomach as a more permanent bandage.

"Don't listen to him," Otto pleaded. "Look what he done to me."

She attempted to soothe him and allay his fears. "I know. Don't you worry, I'll take good care of you." She stood and yelled up the hill at Mac, who was still watching her. "How could you do this?"

"I'm the only law. Saves time."

She looked down at the stricken Otto. He groaned pitiably.

"It's callous and cruel."

"It's practical."

Cupping her hands for more volume she yelled: "Will you shoot me if I take him?"

"Not unless you bring him over here."

"I'm going to write the Canadian government about you."

"Are you pretty?"

"No. It's none of your business." At that she broke off in disgust, mostly aimed at herself for even answering such a silly question. She knelt beside King Otto again. "Can you get on my horse for the ride to Daughton, if I help?"

"Where?"

"All right, Dogtown." She helped him to sit up.

"Oh, no. That's not a friendly place, you don't want to go there."

"It's the closest. And, sir, I'm afraid you'll die if I don't get you there soon. Mustn't be scared, I'll be very careful with you."

He squinted at her again, closing one eye like a pirate. "You some kind of doctor?"

"No, but I've had experience berthing cows and such." She started trying to pull him to his feet, got him more or less upright, and, together, they staggered over to her horse where a new struggle began.

Mac sat on his haunches on the hill and continued to watch them until, eventually, they evanesced in the blue ground mist that came ahead of evening.

Chapter Four

Callie had walked all the way with Otto, now unconscious, tied to her horse. Trudging through the perennial summer mud of the main thoroughfare, she was full of bleary-eyed wonder at the number of people, far more, it seemed, than the ramshackle buildings would shelter. And all the noise and light in this god-forsaken place.

There were the usual businesses—livery stable, general store, an assay office, feed store, a couple of cafés, blacksmith, hotels, boarding houses, saloons, and, of course, whorehouses. Because of the shortage of glass, some had windows composed of the fused bottoms of beer and liquor bottles, giving off an eerie light from within. Spotted here and there among the buildings and behind them were tents, sometimes little colonies of them around a bonfire, men sitting outside, smoking pipes, playing checkers, telling tales of gold and home.

She dragged past what she thought was a hotel, **The Soiled Dove**, on whose porch there reclined a number of painted women who called out to the passing miners enticements, cajolery, barbs, and insults. It was the sense of small-town ritual as much as the gaudy costumes that caught her interest.

The meaning of a lot of what she heard escaped her, but not the tone. Her college, Bowdoin, was a religious school, and Maine pretty much failed as a demimonde, but she had also read Balzac there, and even Zola.

One of the girls spotted her watching them from out in

the dark of the street. "Say, young fella, wanna come up here and sit a spell."

Another nightbird in a rocking chair yelled—"Yeah . . . on her face!"—and they all cackled, not unlike the women with whom Callie was familiar back home at, say, a church or school supper or sewing bee. She had missed the allusion but was struck by this anomaly. Were women the same everywhere?

"Hey, you, kid! Cat got your tongue?"

"I'll give you mine," another added, and they all laughed again.

It had taken this long for Callie to realize that they were actually calling to her, and to remember that she was bringing in a badly wounded man. She picked up speed, and the girls laughed and brayed again, convinced that the "kid" was scared of them.

A gaudy, jerrybuilt theater had someone inside it singing a shaky version of "Un Bel Di" to even shakier piano accompaniment. There was a crowd around a trained bear up ahead; Callie would have loved to be able to stay and see it.

Hurrying past the jail, which was dark, she managed only a glance at the notice on the door: **ANY PRISONER NOT BACK BY SUNDOWN WILL BE LOCKED OUT FOR THE NIGHT**. A couple urged red-blooded young men to enlist to fight the "bullying Spaniard." Another was a Wanted poster for **The Blue Parka Man**, dead or alive, and offered a $1,500.00 reward. The drawing was a generic bandit, totally unrecognizable as Claude. What she noted was the large sum.

In the center of town there were a lot of drunks lying, sitting, or staggering around, some of them Eskimos and Indians. Callie tried to be compassionate, imagining their barren lives.

She started to ask help of three men who seemed relatively well-dressed, but it turned out they spoke only Russian. Wagons, horses, mules, and even a couple of bicycles. A juggler and fire-eater performed outside of another saloon.

"I have a wounded man here. . . ."

At the far reaches of town, a bugler played something similar to "Reveille" and not only received cheers but was accompanied by a chorus of enthusiastic dogs.

"Sir. . . ."

"Git away from me, boy. . . ."

Callie, becoming desperate, checked King Otto to see if he was still breathing—barely. She crossed the street to approach a group gathered around a bonfire listening to a man singing while another accompanied him on the accordion.

Low the blackbird's note and long
Lilting wildly up the glen. . . .

Callie noticed one of the painted women, listening on the fringe, was crying. To her that meant sensitivity, so she made her appeal: "Miss . . . please. . . ."

"It's so sad." The woman wiped her eyes with a dirty but heavily perfumed handkerchief.

"I know, but this man's badly wounded, and I can't get anyone to care. Would you . . . ?"

The woman looked at her intensely. "You're a girl."

"I know, I know that, but, please, he needs a doctor." She pointed to poor Otto, still draped loosely across the back of the worn-out horse that was panting and slobbering.

The whore moved to a man standing nearby wearing a

Western hat and a six-gun with a pearl handle on his hip. "Sweetie, this little girl needs help. Maybe she could use some work, you know. Got all her teeth."

"Her? I can get boys better lookin'." This was said in passing as Jorem Swope was trying to figure out where he might have seen Callie.

"No, you don't understand. This man's been shot, and I can't seem to get anyone to care. Would you help me?"

"Huh?" He squinted in the direction of Otto. "Where'd you find him?" He moved over to grab his former pal by the hair, lifting his head so the firelight fell on his ravaged face.

"Coming here along that border creek." Callie spoke rapidly, breathlessly, as much out of her debilitation as desperation. "He was shot by some crazy man claimed to be a Northwest Mounted Policeman. But, of course, it couldn't have been. I don't know which way to turn. Will you help me, please?"

Jorem grinned. He had filed many of his teeth in imitation of a Bulgarian strongman he had seen in the *Police Gazette* in order to give himself a unique and frightening appearance, and, when he showed his taunting smile, pulling the lips back along the side, it only made him look like a basking crocodile.

"You just see if I don't." He giggled.

Callie didn't get all of this, but she sensed ill-will, and, besides, he looked familiar to her, too. Evil, Reverend Purdy had always preached, was the same everywhere in the world no matter how you dressed it up, and this one practically smelled of brimstone.

He turned to the group around the fire and called them to attention, waving his arms. "Boys! Boys, listen here! Stop the music." It stopped, and there wasn't anyone within earshot who wasn't looking his way.

Irrationally Callie's hopes soared—the poor man was going to be saved!

But Jorem shoved her out of the way to get back to Otto. He again lifted him by the hair and announced: "We got us a better entertainment than that . . . we got us a hangin'!"

There were a few anticipatory whoops at that, but most waited to see who they were hanging. Jorem raised his voice to be heard over the gathering crowd. "This here's King Otto. He jist shot Alibi Johnson up at Forty-Mile and stole his poke. I was there. They been huntin' him for three days."

It turned out that several of the people in the crowd knew or had at least heard about King Otto, and there seemed to be a negative opinion all around.

"Drag him down!"

"Get a rope!"

"Hang the murderin' bastard!"

"I hate krauts!"

The overall atmosphere, nevertheless, was festive as a dozen hands cut Otto loose and dragged him to the ground.

It took Callie a moment to recover from her shock before she fought her way into the crowd, crying: "No! Wait! He's hurt. You can't hang an innocent man. . . ."

She got knocked down for her trouble. People were starting to pour out of neighboring buildings as the mob swelled exponentially. She struggled to get up off the ground but ended by being bumped and jostled all the way out of the crowd.

"Rope! Who the devil's got rope long enough?"

"Please! Help!" Callie continued to plead at the top of her voice, which was nothing against that of the crowd. "Please, you can't do this!"

A voice in a human wilderness, she looked around for

help. Not finding any, she ran down the block to the nearest hotel, Zhang's, straight up the steps, and into the lobby.

There were four hefty, brightly colored whores sitting there with even more brightly colored drinks in their hands, half-bagged, smoking and laughing. One had an opium pipe. Callie, breathing hard, rushed up to the closest and oldest. In her excitement she didn't even notice the enormous, largely exposed breasts and exaggerated paint job.

"Please, madam, would you help me? I need a sheriff or something."

The woman looked at her hazily and drawled: "First of all, honey, I ain't the madam. Tillie!" she screamed, loud enough to make the chandelier tinkle.

Callie, for the first time, recognized where she was and who they were. Looking around in amazement, her jaw dropped.

"What's the carnival goin' on outside?" one of the girls asked.

"They're trying to lynch a man out there."

Callie had barely finished the sentence before all four were up out of their chairs and running, yelping with delight, out the door. It stunned Callie who spun around in confusion and failed to see the buxom Tillie sashay in behind her.

"Well, now, sweetheart, let's see what we got here."

"Who . . . ? Wha . . . ?" She turned back and made yet another plaintive plea for understanding: "THERE'S GOING TO BE A LYNCHING OUT THERE!"

Tillie looked her over appraisingly. "First good news I've had today."

"Good news? They'll kill him! Without even a trial."

"I know, I know, honey, but, you see, if it's not one

thing, it's another, and a lynchin's just real good for business. I don't know what it is about men, but it does seem to get their peckers all bothered."

Callie's shock was cosmic and, at least for the moment, stilled even her activist mouth.

Tillie went on: "Now, lookin' at you. . . . I don't know if you got the muffins for this kind of work, honey, 'less you wanna show me wrong, but it's sure a perky face. With a lotta food and a little cosmetic. . . ."

"If you want to help me, call the sheriff!!" Callie burst out in her face.

Tillie remained calm. "My, you're an excitable little thing, ain't you. Well, we ain't got one."

"I'm not little, and I'm not excited!" Callie screamed. "What's the matter with everyone around here? I want a sheriff!"

A man's voice said: "She told you, we don't have one." He came through a curtain leading to a back hallway, buttoning up the front of his pants, his coat tucked under his arm. Claude Emmett.

Callie turned her head and looked. Claude stopped in his tracks, and his face went perfectly blank. Callie stared for a moment. Tillie was curious about that look, but, since curiosity was not a salubrious quality in her profession, she pushed it away and said about Claude: "If we did, this one wouldn't be here."

He gave her a darting glance that might have killed a more sentient whore, but Tillie just shrugged and murmured: "Pardon me."

Callie was still regarding him quizzically, her whole face scrunched, so he did what came naturally to him, went on the offensive, flashing a smile that could have charmed most women away from hearth and home.

"Can I help you, miss?" he asked sweetly, if in a slightly altered voice.

Callie poured out the whole frantic tale, and Claude listened just as if he cared.

"Is that so?! Shocking. I wouldn't have ever come here if I'd known it was that kind of town." He turned to the madam. "What kind of place is this, Miss Tillie?"

"The kind you can have fun in, blue eyes."

"Not my idea of fun, taking an innocent life," he said sternly.

"I tried to stop them, but they knocked me down," Callie explained. "Are you going to help me or are you a big coward like everyone else in this Sodom?"

Stung, Claude dropped completely out of character for an instant. "Who the hell you calling . . . ?" He stopped himself, took a breath, and reprised the huge smile. "Can't have you thinking that, young miss."

Trapped. Ought to be a way out of this somewhere without playing the fool. There wasn't. Feeling for the Navy Colt in his belt, he allowed grimly: "Can we, Miss Tillie?"

"Claude, you lost your marbles?" the whore said.

"Quite possibly." He drew himself up and stalked out the door. Callie, taken by surprise, jumped to follow.

"Claude!" Tillie yelled after him, "that's all trash out there . . . for this little slip of nothin'?"

Outside, Claude paused and looked at the Bosch-like scene a couple of doors away, drunken miners and their doxies like dancing devils cavorting and shouting around the slack figure of King Otto propped up on another horse. Made skittish by all the excitement, it kept moving around. The hangman was so drunk he couldn't get the rope over an extended beam, which slowed the festivities somewhat. Shots were being fired in the air, quarrels broke out. The only one not overly excited was Otto who gave no sign that there was anything left to hang.

Callie looked expectantly at Claude. "We don't have much time."

"That isn't your pa or anything down there, is it? 'Cause that bunch is a tad ugly."

Callie gave up on him. "That's the limit!" She stomped off down the street. "I'll stop them myself."

Claude watched her and couldn't help admiring the keen, youthful fearlessness, the almost childish gait through the mud, as if she were going to some sort of game, instead of a killing where she could as easily become a victim herself. It was god-damn' annoying.

She didn't go straight to the roiling crowd around King Otto, but to her own horse abandoned in the middle of the street where she fought to get the shotgun out of its carrier.

"Oh, boy," Claude said.

Chapter Five

Claude began to trot and then run, although he couldn't imagine why he should care. There wasn't even the romantic excuse of risking all for a beautiful maiden; all he had seen of this one was a small patch of starved, dirt-covered face in a moving pile of rags. Once he had decided, though, he was impressive, moving into the swirling, fighting mass, thrusting people out of his way with that coolly determined stride that says: Don't tread on the tall man. And, fortunately, people did give way.

Callie, meanwhile, was trying to scuttle in with her shotgun, hoping to reach Otto's side so she could face everyone down with it, but getting nowhere. "Excuse me, sir," didn't seem to have the same effect up here.

"Listen here, boys!" Claude shouted. "Quiet down now!"

Claude thought he knew mobs as well as anyone; he had once talked one out of hanging him, and another actually had hung him. He had seen enough of mobs to lower his estimation of humanity in general.

The thing to look out for was their volatility. They rolled about in any or all directions like quicksilver but with the force of an avalanche, and were capable of taking as victim anything or anyone in their sight without mercy or regret. At least until the next day when it didn't do you any good. And here he was in the middle of one trying to be reasonable, when there was nothing a mob hated worse.

Suddenly there was a loud *bang,* really an explosion, on

the fringe that jarred everybody sober enough to stand—Callie had fired her humungous shotgun into the air to get their attention. It knocked her down, but she sat there, screaming: "Listen to him!"

Everyone ducked; some held their ears, swearing and snarling. She took advantage of the confusion to get up, dive through the crowd, and get close to Emmett.

He flashed her a dirty look but also took advantage of the moment's relative silence. "Boys, you got to listen to me. This is dangerous, what you're doing. And it's gonna come back on you. . . ."

He was interrupted by an outraged cry—"Ow! . . . I been shot!"—from somewhere in the crowd. Then another, as pellets dropped like hailstones on tin roofs and bare scalps.

"God damn, my head's broke. I'm bleedin'!"

"The sky's fallin', boys."

One man went down, then another. A third began to hop around like a one-legged chicken that cursed.

Claude looked at Callie and hissed: "Don't they have gravity in Vermont?"

"Oh, Lord, I didn't think."

"What's wrong with that bitch?"

"That's a boy, and I say shoot the bastard."

Claude drew his own pistol, fired it into the air to draw off the animus of the crowd, and in the brief interim whispered to Callie in no uncertain terms: "Git!"

Now there were a few suggestions that Claude should hang. He glanced at King Otto, propped up in the saddle, and couldn't tell if he were dead or alive. "You can't hang this wahoo, anyway, he's already dead."

Somebody cried out: "We'll hang him live, we'll hang him dead, but by God we're gonna hang the son-of-a-bitch some ways! And you, too, buttinsky."

"What about the miners' court?" Claude demanded, desperately reaching. All he knew was that every town had one. "Somebody get the miners' court over here."

If anyone heard him, no one cared, which was no surprise, and a lot of flushed, agitated faces closed in on him.

"You wouldn't mind your own beeswax, stranger," someone snarled in his ear, but was afraid to grab him.

"He's pard of this other," another said.

And another: "Who is this cheechako, anyhow? Sure's hell ain't no miner. Look at his hands."

Callie had sought sanctuary on the porch of a feed and tack store and from up there could see Claude standing tall in the middle of the maëlstrom. He was suddenly indomitable in her eyes, fearless . . . how could she have been so wrong? Who was he? And then it hit her—*Vermont! He had said Vermont?* Only one person this side of Skagway knew.

A tall, straight-up, bearded man, apparently the only sober one in the crowd, pushed in close behind Claude, who was unaware of him. He remained there, back to back, quiet with a hair-trigger intensity.

If things weren't bad enough, Jorem Swope swaggered into the crowd. "Stand aside."

To an uninformed Claude this was just some arrogant, acned punk shoving rough men aside in a rude manner, and he wondered why they didn't shoot him, or at least knock him down. He got his answer in part when Jorem stopped in front of him and sneered; this bunch would do anything, accept anything, any consequence so long as it promised entertainment.

No, that was unfair, they might have stopped short of roasting babies on spits, but, looking into that wasteland of faces, he would not have been surprised to learn that any one of them, marooned for the winter in some isolated cabin, might not have gnawed on a companion's thigh bone.

Jorem told Claude: "You're either a fool or that bastard's partner in the killin'. Which is it?"

"Mayhap he's the Blue Parka Man," someone else said, and everybody laughed.

Except Callie, looking on. Her eyes had grown enormously large, color came into her pallid, narrowed face, and for the first time since she had come to Alaska she was almost pretty. Unfortunately there was no one there to see it.

Claude looked now at Jorem with absolutely expressionless eyes, which was an expression in itself and an ominous one. If this had been a less primitive young man, he would have seen it.

"You better haul ass, stranger," the kid said, "an' let these here boys git on with their work, or I jist might settle you myself."

Suddenly, and the effect was startling, Claude smiled, but the kind big carnivores show when they're digesting. "Son, I'm sure you're a reasonable man at heart," Claude told him, as if the dripping tusks of a wild boar about to charge could indicate reason.

"I ain't reasonable. I don't even know what it means."

"I tell you, I don't see as how we got any kind of a quarrel here, friend. Seems to me all's called for is . . ."—he looked from face to face, playing the crowd—". . . drinks all around, right, boys?" He added: "This gentlemen here, whoever he is, he's buyin'!"

No one spoke, no one moved.

"How about that?" he added, forcing enthusiasm into his voice without success.

They were waiting for a bigger show—someone dying.

The bearded man moved closer behind Claude. He had

spoken to no one in the crowd nor had he participated in its tumultuous ebb and flow of spleen.

Jorem, not being a man of words himself, had begun doubly to resent all this chatter. "I tell *you* what I'm lookin' at. A yeller dog. A lyin' son-of-a-bitch who keeps on talkin' 'cause he's feared even to run away. I see a kraut-lovin', nigger-kissin', Chinee-lickin' boy-bunger, is what I see."

The crowd dropped into silence like a stone in a bottomless well; this was getting too good to breathe, and better by the minute. Claude smiled again. This time a little sadly, shaking his head. Another bad sign for those with eyes to see. His real concern wasn't Jorem himself, it was what the mob would do if he killed him? Tear him, Claude, apart or carry him off on their shoulders? For some reason he couldn't fathom, all these good citizens seemed to have some sort of twisted respect for this unwashed, squint-eyed, misshapen lethal punk in front of him.

"Sonny, you're pushing me."

Behind him, a little gambler sweating in furs, bent on currying Jorem's favor, pulled out a Derringer and started to point it at Claude's back.

The bearded man, in turn, reached out with one hand and clamped five fingers to his wrist, squeezing the gun out of it as if it was pulp. Simultaneously, with the other hand, he grabbed the assassin's collar and lifted him off the ground to dangle. The little man didn't kick or flail, simply hung there and trembled like dry grass in winter, just trying to stay alive. There were squeaks, whistles, and glugs where his own collar cut into his throat.

Claude heard something going on behind him, but if he took his eyes off Jorem, he was dead anyway, so he would have to trust to Providence.

"Go on, do somethin' 'bout it," Jorem said.

Claude didn't move a muscle anywhere in his body, and he was no longer smiling.

Turning to his audience, a disgusted Jorem said: "He ain't gonna do nothin'. Come on, boys, let's git that murderin' bastard strung." He made the mistake Claude had been unwilling to risk—he started to turn away.

Claude whipped the Navy Colt out of his belt and fired two rapid shots through Jorem's hat, blowing it off his head.

The kid wasn't exactly a virgin in violence; he heard the gun scraping out of the belt, the rustle of clothing as Claude's arm came up, the hammer going back, perhaps even the suspension of breath that smooths the aim, heard them all as a whole indicating menace. He spun back, reaching for his own holstered Old West six-shooter. But by the time he got all the way around, with his pistol approaching his fourth rib, he had lost his hat and was looking down the long barrel and sizable muzzle of the Colt aimed straight between his eyes.

"I'll kill you sure as night," Claude whispered in the sudden vacuum around them.

Slowly the kid put his weapon back into its holster. "God damn you, that was a forty-dollar hat." You could see that he wanted desperately to pick it up to examine it, but now *he* was afraid to look away from Claude. Embarrassed but paralyzed, even his stance was awkward.

Someone in the crowd commented suspiciously on Claude's skill, although in reality the target was only a few feet away. "He's too damn' good with that gun."

Claude, trying to keep as many as possible in front of him, kept the Colt out. "I was aiming for his ear." He glanced around to see if there was anywhere to go, and it wasn't encouraging.

Jorem, too, could play to the crowd. "He took me unawares. You all seen what he did. I never had no fair chance." He turned back to Claude as if the latter was a friendly witness. There was sweat on his forehead now despite the cold, and spittle at the corners of his mouth. "You put away that pistol and I'll fist fight you. You got the belly for that?"

Claude groaned. "Get out of here, jackass."

Jorem put up his arms as if quieting the crowd, although it was already quiet from trying to hear. "I'm challengin' him, you all heard. You won't let him shoot me down like a dog."

Claude stuck his pistol back in his belt. "If that's what you want, boy."

Jorem had started to bounce around in the mud on the balls of his feet with his fists up and elbows down in the boxing stance of the time.

The crowd pulled back to form a rough circle, their collective faces reflecting new hope, becoming almost jovial. People who would bet fortunes in gold on which way a roach might run across a bar would not be denied on this one, and hoarse cries went up.

"Ten on the Swope boy!"

"A hunnert at two-to-one on the cheechako!"

"Who'm I fightin' here, John L. Sullivan?" Claude asked, moving in steadily on his bouncing opponent.

Without ever clenching his fists, he walked right through Jorem's first wild punches, swatting them aside like a cloud of black flies, whipped the Colt back out of his belt in a blur that could not have been tracked even by someone watching for it, and cracked the kid alongside his head with the barrel. Blood came splattering from the scalp in all directions as he toppled, a lightning-struck tree, with no more than a grunt.

Claude looked down at his victim, now lying on his back

with his tongue showing and eyes turned up into his head, with the curiosity of a professional evaluating his work. He seemed satisfied.

"Anybody else here want to box?"

Turning to look at the circle of harsh, flushed faces, he leveled the Colt and pulled a Smith & Wesson out of his belt in back. Unfortunately he was still surrounded, trying to ease away with nowhere to go.

Angry men began to shout curses and brandish guns, clubs, and knives. Someone in the back of the crowd waved a pickaxe back and forth slowly like some large grotesque metronome. A whisky bottle landed at Claude's feet and shattered.

He tried to shout over the noise but couldn't imagine that he was heard. Some were spitting tobacco in his direction when he couldn't afford to duck. A rock struck his forehead and drew a small amount of blood. They wouldn't shoot—no fun in that—unless he did, and therein lay his dilemma. To protect himself in any effective way meant certain death. The circle began to close remorselessly.

Then Callie showed up next to him with the shotgun. She looked terrified and was actually shaking, but her lips were pressed determinedly together. Claude couldn't think of anything to say. The bearded man joined them, back to back, holding a large Webley pistol with lanyard dangling, and forming a desperate three-cornered star.

"Bucko," the bearded man said under his breath.

"Thanks."

Callie tried to say something through her chattering teeth, not so much from fear of being hurt or even killed, but out of revulsion for the idea of killing and the panorama of human depravity surrounding her. Nothing had prepared her for this.

"Let's hang these three with 'um," came a male voice from the crowd.

Claude looked to see who it was, determined to shoot this particular bastard first if it came to that, but couldn't identify him.

"Get out of here," he whispered to Callie.

"No."

All three tensed, sensing yet another change of mood toward increased savagery in the animal body of the mob, if that was possible. Even its collective voice became more strident, cruel, while planks, buck knives, a few guns, and a couple of ropes were hoisted like battle flags to announce its resolution. This time the noose.

"What the hell's going on here?" This voice was different. Chockablock with authority, it sawed through everything in front of it, a voice accustomed to being obeyed. Everyone turned to the porch of the feed store where a short, chesty, bull-necked and black-eyed man with a powerful mustache, wearing a fur coat and derby, stood glowering at the mob. Jude Slocum could have been a Tammany boss, except that as the chief judge of the dreaded miners' court he held life or death over people's heads with the same certainty as a Citizens' Committee of the French Revolution.

Instant quiet, near silence—nothing shuts up a drunk.

"You know we don't brook mob law in this town. If there's any lynching to be done, miners' court'll do it. Get the rope off that man and bring him into the saloon for a proper trial. Somebody find the croaker. Can't have him dying before we hang him. Now git!"

As always, people, even those who are part of an angry gathering, are relieved to have someone take charge, and most of these obeyed with alacrity, lowering or putting their weapons away altogether, moderating their voices to the point of a buzz.

"Come on, snap to it! I'll have every god-damn' one of you up in front of the court. A few more of you dumb bastards kick air and it'd be a nice easy town. Go on!"

He turned on his heel like the former military man he was and set the pace toward the Northern Lights Saloon and courthouse. Otto was carried along behind by the crowd, which promptly lost interest in the other three it had been intent on lynching only moments before.

The bearded man who had risked his life with theirs was gone. "Where the hell?" Claude said, spinning.

"I know who you are," came a voice at his side. Callie started to tell him, but Claude whirled and clamped his hand over her mouth, looking around to see if anyone had heard.

Glaring a warning, he slowly removed his grip. "Princess, I'd keep my speculations to myself, if I was you."

She sputtered: "Princess, indeed! You think talk like that'll turn a plain person's head?"

He looked around again. The crowd had passed on to the saloon, and the few people in sight were either passed-out or hurrying in that direction.

"There's a reward out for you."

He stared hard at her.

"I'm a practical person, without funds, and you are a dangerous criminal," she said almost cheerfully.

By now he looked at her as though he just might have her liver for dinner. "What is it you intend on doing, Miss Fisk? 'Cause there's not a lot of things can get you killed in Vermont, short of putting your head in a thresher, but up here there's a whole bunch."

Callie kept a straight face, but she was enjoying herself

for the first time since she had come to the Northwest. "Oh, you can rest easy, Mister Emmett. It happens to be my misfortune that you saved my life."

Claude began to breathe normally again.

"But just don't you think I admire you."

"Hell, I couldn't afford for you to admire me. Your despising me almost got me hung."

Chapter Six

"Oh, God Almighty, what are you doing in here now?" Claude demanded.

They were at one end of a long barroom. At the other, a hapless King Otto was stretched out, comatose, the bottom half of his long johns pulled down around his ankles, on a pool table covered by sheets that were none too clean. A bucket beside him on the table was already full of bloody rags.

Members of the miners' court, four plus Slocum as the chief justice in the middle, were taking their places on chairs hoisted onto the bar where they would have a certain majesty from the mere fact of altitude. Whisky bottles were placed next to each chair, but in this crowd that did nothing to diminish their loftiness. Also, the fact that their chairs had only a couple of inches leeway on the bar top created a wonderful potential, appreciated by all, for a noisy fall from justice.

There was a great deal of bustle, milling, excited talk resulting in a constant buzz. No one was particularly interested in the prisoner himself, or what was left of him.

"It is a bit . . . close," Callie admitted, looking a little woozy. Actually she was trying to hold her nose without anyone seeing it. "But I'd just like to make sure the trial is fair."

Claude was stunned. *"Fair?"* He pronounced the word as though it had been dipped in skunk bile.

"Maybe someone will do the same for you someday,"

she told him pointedly, and shuffled away.

The "surgeon" working on Otto was at least as scruffy-looking as most of the miners, and almost as drunk. In fact, there was a whisky bottle on the table beside his black bag that he claimed was for antiseptic purposes, and periodically he wiped his hands on his beard while the scalpel clearly had its origins in someone's kitchen. One of the girls had lent her sewing kit.

Two nightbirds, who had neglected to remove their gaudy plumage, were the assisting nurses. One sat on the patient's legs and held up a lantern, as the light in the saloon was none too good. She had trouble sitting still, though, preferring to rock from side to side, singing "Sweet Rosie O'Grady" to herself.

The doctor swore at her perfunctorily, for he was a man who had come to understand that up here you worked with what you had. When he was through, he might feed her some poppy to bring her down, but right now he couldn't risk it. The other sat on the edge of the pool table at the victim's head and applied chloroform by dripping it on her handkerchief.

The patient moaned loudly. "Hold him, god dammit!" the doctor snarled. "And quit bouncing him."

"Keep it quiet," Slocum called from his lofty perch. "We're trying to have an orderly trial here."

"Don't give him too much of that damn' chloroform, woman," the doctor snapped at his anesthesiologist.

She, too, was unimpressed—"Say, I use this stuff for whoopee."—and took a pleasurable little sniff herself to prove the point.

The doctor shook his head and kept cutting.

The trial began while the defendant lingered closer to death than life. There was an empty chair with King Otto's cap signifying the defendant himself. Everyone else crowded around this and another chair for the witnesses. An Eskimo lay unconscious by the door, clutching in an iron grip that no one had been able to break a bottle of homemade liquor the miners called hooch. Smoke-clogged air that had been blue was going to charcoal black, which caused endless hacking and hawking but also had the advantage of co-opting the many other even less pleasant odors.

Jorem Swope, his head bandaged, stood before the witness chair and spoke in a loud voice. "The old man, Alibi Johnson, he didn't even have no gun, an' he was sleepin' anyways. An' this bastard here . . ."—he indicated the cap on the chair—"kilt him like a dirty dog. No chance at all to defend hisself like a man. I seen it all. An' it was horrible to see."

The crowd growled and shouted their disapproval of shooting people while they were asleep.

Slocum reached down to bang on the bar at his feet with a bung starter. "We're gonna have order in this court!"

Other members of the court were taking advantage of the break to refresh themselves. The bartenders could scarcely keep up with demand, and one had already sent for his nephew and cousin to come and help. Even the piano player took the excitement as a cue to start playing. Slocum squelched that by fining him five dollars for disturbing a court in session and promptly contributed it to the liquor fund, a vastly popular judgment.

"All right, Mister Swope," Slocum went on, "answer the court this . . . if the victim was sleeping, and didn't have a gun, who shot the defendant over there? You?"

"Ah. . . .uh . . . that was some miner or t'other. Caught

him comin' outta the tent, you see, after hearin' these screams of helplessness."

The judge to the right of Slocum, an older man with a beard that ended in his lap, asked: "He was sleepin', the victim, but he screamed?"

Jorem appeared to be irritated by the question. "You wake up when you're shot."

"Then how does this Otto get away with a bullet in his gizzard, an armed miner in front of him, and you runnin' all 'round there?"

Jorem had to think even harder, something he had not anticipated, and was increasing his resentment geometrically. The only way he could maintain control was to keep a mantra in his head—*Daddy is comin', Daddy is comin'.*—as if pronouncing doom on the entire territory.

The ugly scowl was natural, beyond his power to moderate. "Well, . . . I didn't have no gun 'cause I was . . . shavin', you see. An' the miner's gun, it jammed up on him after the one shot. So then Otto jist knocked him down and run right over him. He's real strong."

"Not currently," Slocum observed, looking to the far end of the barroom. He called out: "How's he doing, Doc?"

"Still breathing. Kinda."

"All right. We got another witness here. Bob Fairly tells me he heard of this killing of ol' Johnson over at Forty-Mile. Come forward and address the court, would you, Bob. You all know Bob."

A clerkish-looking man, or at least one of the very few in the room wearing spectacles but also city clothes, including an almost fresh striped shirt, a vest, and sleeve guards. Fairly stepped in front of Slocum and turned to address the crowd as if they were his audience. He seemed both nervous, clearing his throat, and pleased to be the center of things for once.

"I sure did, Jude . . . Your Honor. Man came in my store yesterday, he told me of it. He surely did." Fairly hesitated, then blurted: "Only he said there were *two* men doing the robbing and the killing." He moved a step away from Jorem, not daring to look at him.

A hush of expectancy immediately came over the court, proof that the onlookers were deeply involved in the drama of it.

Slowly the judges turned and looked down at Jorem, standing in front of them. "Mister Swope," Slocum said. "Two men?"

Jorem stuck out his chin at them and answered defiantly: "There mighta been." He glared around the room in some desperation. "Fact is," the kid said, sucking it up, "I believe it's that sum'bitch over there." He pointed straight at Claude. "You all seen 'im buffalo me." He indicated his bandaged head and tried to look aggrieved.

He had succeeded in focusing attention on Claude, who had deliberately remained in the back of the crowd with his cap tipped over his eyes. As everyone turned to look at him, he flashed a reproving glance at Callie, one of those too-sweet smiles that means "I'd really like to kill you."

Slocum fixed him with his formidable, black-browed gaze and ordered him forward. Reluctantly, having no choice, Claude moved slowly to confront the court. There were grumbles and resentful looks when he was recognized as the man who had interfered with their fun earlier.

"I seen you around somewhere. Who are you, son?" Slocum asked.

"Name's Claude Emmett from Oregon, Your Honor. New to these parts."

"Must be, to assault the youngest boy of John Brown Swope."

That explained a lot, but Claude thought it better to lie and play the innocent for as long as he could. "Never heard of the gentleman."

"You will," Jorem sneered at him.

"Just tried to impart a little Christian charity to an unreasonable man, Your Honor. Had to shoot his hat off to get his attention."

"Musta shot a little low, by the look of him," the judge on the other side of Slocum said, and got a good laugh from the crowd. He was a young man in old clothes, a string bean with a long neck sticking out of a faded cravat. His worn face bore almost as many knobs and scars as his hands.

Jorem Swope was not amused and glared at the judge while grabbing at the bandage on his head and yanking it off. It started to bleed again, but death was preferable to mockery. If the old man heard about it, he might as well be dead.

"Now, there you are," Claude went on. "See, how that happened, he wanted to box with me after that, so I had to calm him down some, that's all. I know you gentlemen pride yourselves on a nice quiet town."

That, too, got some laughs and ironic comment from the crowd, but Slocum's keen eyes narrowed, and he leaned down over his knees. "Wouldn't be soapin' us a little, would you?"

"I'm the one called for a miners' court," Claude reminded them.

"That's to your credit. Also saved your neck. What do you do for kit and keep?"

"Oh, I been an apothecary, cowboy, railroad man, sailor.

Clerked in a bank in Seattle last."

"We don't have a lot of banks," Slocum stated. "Fact, the actual number is none. So I repeat my question."

"Thinking of doing a little prospecting, I guess."

"I'd recommend it. We don't like to see a man shoots as good as you unemployed. Now, what do you know about the matter at hand?"

"Only what I seen happened here an hour ago." He looked around, suffering a last minute panic at the thought that Callie might have left. "See, I was south of here on the trail where I rescued that young woman back there"—he pointed and smiled vengefully at where she too was trying to avoid scrutiny—"from a blue ticket trying to rip her clothes off her."

That naughty idea brought guffaws from the crowd, men and women who were used to men, and a blush that seemed to suffuse Callie's whole person. She looked around as if there might be some way to avoid the attention of everyone in the room, but, of course, it was impossible.

Actually, while Claude was enjoying the opportunity to embarrass her, he had to worry that she might not, out of spite or God knows what female caprice, deny his story. He had to hope that she had seen how quickly a man could get hung up here.

Another thought intruded; that blush showed her face to him for what was really the first time, or at least in a new light. Still dirty and ravaged, but, was it possible, she might be almost . . . pretty? Maybe he had been up here too long.

"You there, young woman," Slocum called out to her, "is that true?"

She stole an opportunity to flash Claude her own look, one of primal, undying hatred, the likes of which she would never have thought herself capable a month earlier. Its message: "Maybe I'll say yes and maybe I won't, sweat a little, you bastard."

Meanwhile, the boys poured out their wit with loud remarks such as: "Bet he took his sweet time savin' her." Or: "Maybe he didn't know that was a female."

Callie was too preoccupied to hear. Sitting down with her hands primly in her lap, feet and knees tightly together, she put on her schoolmistress, intensely sincere persona and looked up at the court with an expression that was the equivalent of the first robin in spring. Yet when she tried to speak, it was to discover her mouth dry and nearly inoperable.

"It's true, Your Honor," she got out finally, sweating and stammering in a rusty, small voice. It seemed bizarre and a little unnerving to address a judge when he was sitting atop a bar with a pistol on his hip, a bung starter in his hand, and in a room she would not even have been allowed to enter back home.

"What? Speak up."

She almost shouted, getting another laugh: "He's telling the truth, except the blue ticket man was trying to kill me. At least *I* thought so."

"In that case . . . ," Slocum said in a booming, authoritative voice before remembering the four other judges on the panel. He stopped while they put their heads together for about thirty seconds. He resumed his lofty aspect and pronounced: "In that case, the court finds the defendant, known in these parts as King Otto, alone in being guilty as charged, and sentences him to be hanged in the morning if he can stand or sit. May God have mercy on his miserable soul. Further, Mister Emmett is cleared of any connection with this case, but ordered to pay for Mister Swope's hat."

The crowd roared in all different directions and colors,

some excited, others disappointed. Most were just yapping at the moon. Jorem Swope was confused as to exactly where he stood.

Several guns were discharged until Slocum swung at one reveler with the bung starter and broke his arm. The celebrant went down and was carried over to await the doctor's ministrations. They had to give him his own bottle of whisky to shut him up.

Callie, frowning, fought through to the bar to beard the court. "Just a minute, Your Honors. Begging your pardon, but this isn't fair. . . ."

Claude, having wisely retreated to the fringe again, murmured an appeal to heaven: "Fair?"

Slocum looked down as one might when plagued by an obstreperous child.

Callie was not intimidated. "No one's asked me to testify." Having said that, she attempted to look defiant.

"You already did," Slocum complained. "You said about that dubious stranger back there"—once again everyone in the room turned to look at Claude—"he was south of here when Mister Swope says he was t' the north killing Alibi Johnson in the company of our defendant, now convicted and condemned. I think that's quite enough testimony from one person. 'Sides, trial's over."

"I want to testify again."

"Why?"

Someone in the crowd called out: "That's the dumb cow with the scatter-gun."

"I have important information for the court," she persisted.

"You're a woman," one of the judges, an old man with crossed eyes, pointed out.

"So was your mother," Callie shot back, amazed at her

own audacity, but not displeased that it earned her a few raucous laughs. She was smart enough to know that she couldn't handle Slocum that way. "I'm also the person who found that poor soul . . ."—she pointed in the direction of the ongoing surgery, but couldn't bring herself to look—"over there."

Slocum didn't bother to look, except to glare at Callie from the olive pits on either side of his nose. "This 'poor soul' is well known to us, young lady. King Otto is a liar, a thief, and a skunk. All them before you were even born. He was part of Soapy Smith's gang in Skagway, robbing the poor, the infirm, and the mental deranged, only *they* found him too wicked."

The old judge overlapped to put in: "Man who'd steal your dog while you was sleepin' on him, fleas and all."

"If there was an ounce of reindeer jerky between twelve orphans and starvation," Slocum went on, straightening again to appear more magisterial, "he'd spit on it to give 'em the typhoid fever. In short, his death will cause chaos in heaven 'cause hell won't have him. That's your 'poor soul.' "

The bearded one said—"Not to mention he's ugly as a pickled moose nose."—as he spat into a spittoon 'way down on the floor. No one seemed to mind the splash.

The crowd applauded and yelled, some of the remarks aimed at Callie, until Slocum reminded them that there would be no unseemly conduct, particularly coarse language, directed toward ladies in his court.

Some of the whores found that hilarious. Slocum banged the bar hard and glared at them. "I said *ladies!*"

Since practically everyone in the room worked for him, owed him money, or shared a claim with him, they could be tamed. Up to a point.

In the face of all the hostility, Callie burst out: "I . . . I . . . I'm sorry, Your Honor, but I've been to Bowdoin College and studied the opinions of Justice Oliver Wendell Holmes. . . ."

Someone shouted—"We're sorry, too."—and got a rousing laugh.

Callie plunged on over the precipice. "And I'm sure you wouldn't want a standard of justice here that was any less."

The old judge said—"Why not?"—exchanging sour looks with his confreres.

Finally Slocum said wearily: "Go on, young lady."

"If the evidence against the defendant is based on the statement of that terrible man over there . . ."—she pointed to Jorem—"saying how Mister Otto was shot while robbing a miner at some place called Forty-Mile, well, I'm here to tell you he's prevaricating. Because I found the defendant myself right after he'd been fired upon . . ."

Otto gave up a horrible groan that made even some of the more hardened miners and sharpers wince.

". . . by a man claiming to be a member of the Canadian Mounted Police who is nothing more than a bully or a lunatic." She sucked in air. "Finally, let me say, I'm a schoolteacher who always tries to be fair and tell the truth. Thank you."

"Did you see the defendant shot?" Slocum asked, no less fatigued.

"Well, no . . . but I had a discourse with the man who'd done it. He was completely unashamed."

"But you didn't *see* it?"

"Mister Otto told me."

"*Mister* Otto is a confirmed liar."

The cross-eyed judge, who had appeared to be nodding off throughout the entire proceeding, suddenly came to life.

"Listen here, a lot of the men in this barroom, where no respectable lady . . . and I can't say that's you from the look of you . . . but where no respectable lady should be anyway, they come to the Klondike to remove themselves from the likes of women who been to universities just so's they can talk us to death. And VOTE!"

That would have earned a standing ovation if everyone hadn't already been standing. Save Slocum, the other judges shouted—"Amen!"—and the harangue was followed by a lot of cheering and hooting at Callie. The piano player struck up "Rally 'Round the Flag," and a couple of drunks in the back tried to answer with "Dixie" to more hooting and some booing and even a thrown bottle.

Slocum saw that things could get out of hand again just when he had them in hand. "All right, all right, settle down and shut up." He raised himself and his voice to make some headway against the disorder. "The judgment stands. Again! Therefore, this young lady who brought all this up stands indicted of perjury. Trial to be held in this court at five o'clock tomorrow."

Another cheer went up. It was just as loud, but, at least, he had reinstituted a genial atmosphere. Callie tried to shout her protest, but it was swallowed up in the noise and confusion. Somebody shouted up to Slocum that the next day was Sunday.

Slocum looked down pointedly at Callie and said: "That's all right, by then she'll probably've fled this jurisdiction, anyway."

Callie shouted back—"I will not!"—but no one heard her or cared to hear further from her. The show was over.

Some members of the crowd began to drift out, and others bellied up to the bar, or just stood in groups and argued.

Then a tall, bearded man, the one who had saved Claude's bacon back on the street, reappeared out of nowhere and marched up to where the judges were beginning their descent. He put up a hand and demanded to be heard.

"The young lady's right. I shot him."

Chapter Seven

Everyone within hearing froze, one judge with a foot on the chair he was using as a ladder.

"And who in the name of Lucifer are you?" Slocum asked, frustrated. "We got to end this damn' trial sometime before winter sets in."

The stranger pulled off his beard and let it drop. What was left was a full black mustache. "You know me, Mister Slocum."

"I surely do, and I wish I didn't."

Callie's mouth dropped open and stayed that way. Claude laughed when he looked at her. She caught on and slammed her jaw shut.

Turning to address the curious miners, once more gathering around, the stranger announced: "Sergeant Clarence McDonald. Her Majesty's Royal Canadian Mounted Police."

An ugly sound arose from the lingering crowd, something in which they were well-practiced by now. Slocum barked at his fellow judges and prodded them back atop the bar. "I know, I know," he told them, "it's over, only it's not over. It's never gonna be over. Back up there and do your duty. Maybe we'll hang somebody yet." It was important to keep up morale.

People even came back in off the street, along with some newcomers.

"Court's back in session on the trial that never ends. Say your piece, Mister Mountie, and say it quick. This court and everybody else is getting damn' sick of all this."

Mac looked around, standing almost at parade dress, defiant in his professional way, staring hard into eyes just as hard and less constrained. "In pursuant of my duties as an officer of the law I shot Harold King Otto early in the afternoon of the Twenty-Third of May, Eighteen Ninety-Eight, that's yesterday, for unlawfully entering upon the sovereign soil of the Dominion of Canada."

"That the only reason you shot him?" the youngest judge asked him uncomprehendingly.

"No, also because he was no damned good. If the ladies will excuse me."

"These ladies here will," Slocum said, looking out on a garden of whores' plumage. "And nobody's gonna argue with your description of the defendant, I grant you that."

"That's the bastard shot my toe off," someone called out, pointing angrily at the Mountie.

"You got your nerve mister," another said almost to his face.

The new mob was finding the court a little too patient and overly judicious.

"You're on our ground now, you sum'bitch!"

Slocum banged the bung starter several times. "Hold on there, silence in the courtroom." He looked down at Mac. "Maybe you better tell us what you're doing here in that rig?" He pointed to the beard on the floor.

Mac hesitated, seemingly a little self-conscious.

Callie pushed closer.

"Tell the truth, where I live on the border, there's a lot of miles of nothing behind me and nothing in front but Dogtown. Sometimes I just . . . crave a face, so I come over."

That tended to throw a lot of the listeners off course.

Slocum cleared his throat. "I guess you know you're taking a considerable risk showing yourself here."

Mac looked around for Callie and finally spotted her. "I could do no less for that brave young lady."

Callie's mouth had closed, but it popped open again. She started to express her amazement to whoever was standing next to her, the way she might have in Vermont, and found it was Claude again, but spoke anyway: "I never heard such a thing. He must be mad."

"Wouldn't surprise me."

Slocum gave it his best stentorian manner and voice. "All right, the court has heard all the evidence . . . again! . . . and will come to a decision." More quietly, to Mac standing just below and in front of him, he added: "My advice to you, Mister Mountie, is to take your bushwhackin' ways back across that border, P.D.Q. I'll give you till noon."

Mac nodded stolidly while the court put their heads together for a perfunctory minute.

This time Slocum stood up and waited for silence. "The court has got yet another decision in this matter, the People of Daughton versus . . ."—he looked down at Mac—"what'd you call him . . . Harold?"

Mac nodded solemnly again.

"The People versus Harold King Otto. Said son-of-a-bitch is declared innocent for lack of evidence and is hereby ordered to vacate the premises of said city of Daughton in the Territory of Alaska, U.S. of A., as soon as he can walk, crawl, or ride, never to return." The bung starter came down with a loud crack, splintering the edge of the bar, and Slocum shouted: "This is final!" Then he remembered something. "Oh, by golly. Wait a minute, listen here! The management . . . that's me . . . wants to mention that The

Petite Sisters Pickering will be here for an engagement beginning Sunday week with their own musical accompaniment. Court's dismissed."

Paradoxically, but not surprisingly, the crowd decided that the show had had a long enough run, were bored with it, and cheered the court's decision lustily. Especially when Slocum, a sagacious man who always hedged his bets, bought a round for the house.

Amidst the general uproar Callie's delighted squeal was barely heard, but she jumped up and down like a child and ended up giving Claude a hug—simply because he was standing next to her, and not for long once she realized what she was doing.

He grinned, enjoying both her exuberance and the embarrassment it cost her.

"I . . . I . . . didn't know it was you," she said.

"Say, you're not real homely, after all."

Callie's face started to drop open again, but she was determined to break herself of that habit and caught it in time.

"In fact . . . ," Claude tried to continue.

Instead she cut him off. "I'm sure where you come from, Mister Emmett . . . the Nether Regions would be my guess . . . there are people there ignorant enough to think that was a compliment. But I don't happen to be one of them."

"There, you see, that's what women do. I didn't mean it like that."

Young Jorem Swope, behind them, was setting off on a spectacular tantrum. He had slammed a bottle onto the floor and was dancing his fury in the débris. "Damn you all to perdition!" he screamed. "Makin' a fool and a liar outta me! You're all gonna pay when my folks git here."

People near enough to hear developed long faces and avoided each other's eyes. A circle of quiet rippled out from the tantrum. Jorem loved having an effect.

"That's right. My daddy's comin' to rule over you. Been made a judge. How you like them apples? Won't be no more shithead miners' court to take the word of a little slut like that. . . ."

Callie had never attacked anyone in her adult life, but then neither had she been called a slut before and hard times did seem to be having their effect on her. She let out an angry yell and started to rush at her accuser, but Claude grabbed her arm going by and held her back. He intended to go after Jorem himself, but this cost him his opportunity.

Instead, Mac appeared from nowhere, as he had a habit of doing, and merely reached out a long arm and large fist. It slammed Jorem right on the chin, sending a tooth flying, blood spraying. The victim didn't fall backwards so much as hurtle over a chair and into the wall. By the time he slid to the floor, he was unconscious, bleeding from the chin and mouth, eyes again rolled up into his head.

"Don't you know a lady when you see one?"

Claude, next to him, looked down, shook his head. "That boy is paying for his sins tonight."

People gathered around, but no one wanted to get too close.

Callie had never gone through four distinct emotions in a single day; now she had gone from anger to shock to horror to delight in seconds, so that her blood didn't know which way to flow. Of course, she tried to hide the delight.

Slocum had pushed his way through the crowd around the fight and was behind them. "If you had trouble before, Mister Mountie, you got a wagonload now. There's more Swopes than the Mongol horde. The old man was sired on Salome out of Beelzebub. If he's been made judge here, I'll wave to you from the next gibbet."

"Who the dickens are these Swopes, anyways?" Callie whispered aside to Claude.

"That was as good a description of them as you'll hear right there."

Slocum, who still had his long-handled bung starter with him, raised it on high, waggled it, and shouted: "The verdict was innocent! The defendant is free to go!"

The doctor shouted back—"He just went!"—and everyone turned to the forgotten end of the room where they were drawing a tablecloth over the deceased. The saloon porter set to work cleaning up the unholy mess, dumping some of it into the spittoons. "I think nursie gave him too much whoopee," the doctor added.

The anesthesiologist was proud of her work. "You old sot, *you* killed him."

Nobody cared except Callie, who burst into tears at the announcement.

Mac had struck Jorem to protect her honor, so she chose his shoulder on which to pour out her grief. His large frame enfolded her, and he murmured sweet reassurances, calling her "lass," which somehow sounded soothing.

"I tried so hard to save him. It's so cruel up here. . . ."

Mac patted her and grinned over her shoulder at Claude who, if it had been he, would have reminded her yet again that she was talking about the scum of the North, and, if there was a God, the son-of-a-bitch would have been dancing on hot coals years ago.

When she broke away to get a damp cloth from the bar with which to wipe her face, Claude asked sourly: "How'd you get her to do that?"

"The Scots are a quick and ready race, bucko," Mac replied.

"You'd better be, *bucko,* to get out of this town alive."

"I can't let 'em see a Mountie run, can I?"

"You let 'em see too much already."

Callie, returning from the bar wiping her face, sensed something. "You two seem to be getting along."

"Why wouldn't we?" Mac asked, throwing his arms around an old friend.

"You pious old bastard," Claude said, while they pounded each other's backs and punched shoulders.

Callie was bewildered. Fortunately she was getting used to it, and, lately, the normal had begun to seem abnormal, which was obviously normal in Dogtown.

"I don't need your help, either of you. I can find a place to sleep on my own."

"You're flat out broke," Claude said. "Look at you. Look at that damned poor thing you call a horse." He pointed back at the stable where they had just left her nag.

"I suppose I have to get used to your cursing."

"It's not safe for you out here, wandering around, miss," Mac said, his arm sweeping half the compass. "A fine, educated female like yourself needs to be snug inside somewhere."

Dogtown was finally closing down. The only sounds of hilarity came from the Northern Lights Saloon where the trial had been held. The streets were largely empty except for the sleeping drunks, some of whom would be dead by morning, either from hooch or exposure for the nights could still turn bitter. A singing Irishman came along on a staggering mule, leaning over its neck to offer it whisky from a bottle. In the distance there were two gunshots and then someone screaming. A dog joined in, howling. Callie shuddered.

Claude and Mac waited her out.

"I am tired." Having admitted it to herself, her whole body gave in and sagged piteously. "Maybe. . . ."

"No maybes about it," Claude said. "I'm taking you to Tillie's, cleanest place in Dogtown, change the sheets twice a day. Come on." He put his hand under her arm, but Mac got a hold of the other one and wouldn't let go.

"Hold on. That's no fit place for a decent little girl. . . ."

Her strength renewed by frustration, Callie yanked free and spun to confront both of them. "Will you two stop it! I am not little or helpless. As far as staying in a . . . uh . . . house of ill repute, well, I've been to college and smoked cigars. I know a lot. You might say I am something of a woman of the world. I'll get along fine."

Mac sighed with concern. "No, the lass's spoken. We have to respect that. You give her your Thirty-Eight, though."

He put his arm around her and began to lead her up the street toward Zhang's. She allowed it. She liked it. And he was a Mountie after all, if somewhat odd.

Claude, following, watched them uncomprehendingly. Trying to make up ground, he assured Callie: "You tell anybody bothers you we'll be around to kill 'em in the morning."

Mac, actually looking at Zhang's, again had misgivings. "You sure?" Claude would have spoken, but Mac held up his hand to stop him and warned Callie: "Don't listen to that one, he's no respect for decent women."

"Maybe that's why she likes me. And keep your straight-laced snout outta this."

"I'll fall down right here, if I don't find a bed real soon. You're sure Miss Tillie'll have one?"

"Just tell her, on our say so," Claude insisted.

"You two seem to know her awfully well." Fortunately

she didn't expect an answer. "Well, I'm going in. Thank you for . . . everything." In a kind of flustered spasm she darted a kiss onto the cheek of each. "There! I've never kissed two men on a single night. But then I've never done anything on a single night."

She turned and actually ran to the hotel with all the verve and carelessness of a colt.

"That lass's a mite unusual," Mac said, watching her go.

"Amen."

Chapter Eight

The beds were all busy, but fortunately the bathtub was of a size to handle large men. Unfortunately there was a large man bathing in it. He was summarily ejected. Callie forgot how tired she was long enough to scour it thoroughly before adding blankets and a pillow. A certain amount of scrunching was required, but sleep came anyway.

Then in the spree-dawn hours there came an obnoxious pounding at the door followed by a slurred voice: "Maisie, you plump little partridge . . . come out, honey . . . come out and play."

Callie groaned and fought to roll over onto her back. Her own voice was sleep sodden and may have sounded a false note of sensuality. "Go away. I'm asleep."

"Oh, sweetheart . . . won't you be my honeybee? I got a sweet little stinger . . . *big* stinger!"

"Go away! I'm not your honeybee."

"Yes, you are."

"I'm from Vermont."

"Who cares? Baby needs you ba-a-d. If you don't come out and wrap yourself around him like a honeycomb, he'll have to shoot hisself. Please?"

"All right."

The man outside began to sing "Pretty Redwing" loudly and badly.

Callie heaved herself out of the bathtub—she was sleeping in her pungent clothes, just in case—found Claude's gun, and groped her way to the door. Finding that the chain was on, she opened it a crack. "Here," she said, "use this."—and, holding it awkwardly with two hands, thrust the muzzle through the opening.

That brought instant sobriety as her suitor let out a little yelp of fear and backed away. "All right, all right! Heck, if that's how you feel." She could hear him padding away down the hall, grumbling: "At least my wife could cook."

Perhaps it got around, but no one else came to the door the rest of the night.

In the morning a cleaned-up, gussied-up Callie rocked on the front porch between two of the girls, Vera and Angie, while they watched Dogtown society on their Sunday morning parade. "Health walks" during the short summer were all the vogue.

"Good morning, ladies," a fellow practitioner said, strolling in her finery and twirling her umbrella as if she were in Central Park. Carrie's companions nodded idly and went on rocking. Rocking chairs were considered good for keeping the glands flowing, hence every bordello had them.

Some men went by, grinning evilly and making remarks that went over Callie's head, the exact meaning, anyway. The "girls" beside her took it in stride and smiled back their insincerity.

"I don't think those men were very nice," Callie offered tentatively.

"Look around you, honey," Vera said. She had an eye patch and an ice pack on her head, but was otherwise dressed for company. "Men got the guns, the gold, and the big muscles. All us poor women's got's the joy tube. They can be anything they want. Them that has gits!" She spat off the porch by way of punctuation.

"Yes, but women are smarter because they *don't* have

those things. At least in Vermont."

Angie hadn't said much, pulling slower and slower and slower on her opium pipe, which Callie took for funny-smelling tobacco. But now she spoke up emphatically on a subject that could obviously energize even an addict. "Doesn't do us no good. You stay up here, kid, and you'll end like alla us. Starin' at the ceilin', whistlin' 'Dixie' or listenin' to the ice break up while some unwashed hippopotamus primes your pump and belches in your face."

Callie couldn't entirely keep the revulsion off her own face, but she made sure it didn't remain there long; she was working hard at being both polite and worldly. But she couldn't keep the firmness out of her voice. "I won't. I've got an iron will."

Another fair Cypriot swayed past and said a lilting hello.

"One of Flora's girls," Vera said, " 'the Virgin.' "

Callie didn't want to say the word, but she couldn't help stammering: "The . . . why . . . do they call her that?"

"They say she seen one, oncet," Vera said logically.

Angie had grown languid again, but managed a cackle.

Callie's expression brightened. "Here they are!"

Coming down the center of the street, the safest place to walk on a Sunday morning, when people were cleaning out stables and emptying chamber pots, were Claude and Mac. Both had been to the barber, bathed, and put on clean clothes, Claude in buckskins and Mac wearing his uniform pants and a colorful Indian-made sweater. The two of them, tall, stalwart, bushy-tailed, and full of promise, a maiden's dream.

"You been here a day and you got two like them?" Vera said in awe.

"Uhn-huh," Callie replied absently, standing, beaming simply because she had never been in this position in her life and wanted to enjoy it even if it turned out they wanted nothing else to do with her and would walk right past. "I think so."

It almost happened the way she had feared, for they didn't recognize her. She had put on a dress. Granted it was calico, but still it felt like a ball gown. One of the girls had fitted her with a pair of cheap earrings, her first ever, and a necklace. She had tried on some cosmetic and let her hair be pulled back with a pretty ribbon to keep it in place. The only thing she forgot was to bite her lips and give them color.

Claude and Mac had puzzled, unbelieving looks as they approached Zhang's. Callie waved and jumped down to meet them where they stood rooted in amazement.

Up on the porch Vera wondered: "You think maybe we are smarter in Vermont?"

A photographer had set up in the center of town, dollar a photo. An excitable little man who bounced around like a human cricket, inveigling, exhorting, and doing a good business amongst the fallen women despite the fact that his only backdrop was a big gaudy view of a canvas seashore.

Callie wondered where the girls might be willing to send a photo of themselves in their fallen state. For one giddy moment she fantasized borrowing some gaudier clothes, posing provocatively with a couple of the girls, and sending it to Papa. The mere idea was so exciting it made her head reel. But what would Mama think, a country woman not given to foolery? Somehow life never seemed to be on the side of revenge.

Mac looked at her quizzically.

Recovering, she decided that what she *really did want* was a photograph of herself with her two gentlemen. When would that come again? Claude said it was against his profession, and Mac wasn't sure it was a good thing for him, either. What if Claude got caught and hung, and there's a picture extant of them carrying on together?

Callie begged; she wanted it for when she was alone in the gold fields. What if she was freezing in a blizzard and this was the last sweet memory she had to cling to? What if she got caught by a polar bear . . . ?

They agreed, if only to shut her up. People gathered around in the middle of the street to watch. Fortunately the photographer had a false mustache for Claude, and both men pulled their caps down to shadow their eyes. Still, when the flash went off, it caught one of those quintessential-time-of-our-lives pictures, the men very dignified, J. P. Morgan and Andrew Carnegie or equally Butch and Sundance, Callie breaking with the standards of the time by linking her arms with them, grinning at the camera and fate. A moment they all knew would never come again.

Afterwards, over a second cup of coffee in a café, Mac began to think about getting back to his post on the border. Claude wouldn't say where he was going, naturally, but maintained it was important that he get there. Both asked if they could look Callie up next time they came to Daughton?

She gave them a disgusted look. "You really didn't believe me about my going prospecting, did you? You just went along, humoring me like a little child."

"You know anything about it?" Claude asked, making no attempt to disguise his skepticism.

"I have a book from the Putney Library. Tells you everything you need to know."

"I doubt it."

Mac asked how she was going to get mining equipment, if she was broke?

"My grandfather's lucky gold piece worth fifty U.S. dollars."

"I'll be damned," Claude said. "You let us think you were penniless."

"I was saving it for this." She added defensively: "It was a white lie."

"How come nobody took it before now?"

"I kept it in . . . a very personal place."

"Do you know what to get?" Mac asked more kindly.

"Since it isn't very much money, I suppose I'll have to start by panning. Poor a way as that is."

"Fifty dollars isn't enough," Claude said. "And don't ask me to stake you. My conscience wouldn't let me."

"Don't worry, I'd sooner jump off Pike's Rock."

"When're you planning on going, Miss Callie?" Mac asked.

"Now." She smiled complacently.

"It's the middle of the day on Sunday," Mac pointed out.

"If I'd gone sooner, I would have missed this nice morning. Besides, you're both leaving, what do you care?"

"You'd best get that bee out of your bonnet, missy. You're not going anywhere," Claude said definitively.

"What the hell you mean by telling us there's no mining equipment," Claude growled at the clerk behind the counter.

The poor man looked like a sparrow, all beak and no chin, receding hair, small of stature and presence. He was frightened enough, but presented a problem for the boys—too little and ineffectual to beat up in front of Callie.

"Look around, sir. There's nothing here."

All three looked with him as he indicated. The store was

crowded with a considerable variety of goods, but not even the most basic sort of mining equipment: shovel, pick, pan.

"Where's the boss, where's Fairly?" Mac demanded.

"Went for a . . . buggy ride . . . after the church meeting."

"Fairly doesn't have a buggy." Claude then asked: "So what's he know we don't?"

The little man looked around, then went to the window and looked out. "Somebody come in this morning, when we were opening up, and took all the mining equipment there was."

"So . . . who was it?" Claude said, leaning in on him.

Callie protested: "You're frightening the poor man."

"I sure as hell hope so."

Mac swept some canned peas off the counter with his large paw.

The clerk tried to speak, but it was as indecipherable as the chatter of squirrels.

"Sir," Callie said, "please tell us where it's gone. I'm running out of money, and the people back home are counting on me."

"Tell the lady!" Mac bellowed past her, and Claude pulled out his big Colt to scratch his ear with the muzzle.

"They forbade me to tell."

"I unforbid you," Claude told him.

"The . . . the . . . Swope brothers. *All four of them!*"

"Those silly Swope people again," Callie said.

Chapter Nine

"I don't think they should let a poor dumb animal into a saloon."

"One of the best customers they got," Claude told her, feeding the burro standing at their table from a bottle of beer.

"That can't be good for him." Callie was drinking coffee, although the rest of the place, the Northern Lights again, was filled with hearty imbibers and raucous noise in the early afternoon. "What's his name?"

"Wise Mike."

"He doesn't look too smart to me."

"Oh, I don't know, been drinking here for years and never bought a round yet."

Callie thought she shouldn't laugh at that, but did.

Mac seemed to have been regarding the premises with some affection. "Someday I'll own a place just like this. And it'll never be empty, if I have to give the drink away."

"You want to be a saloonkeeper?" Callie said, a little shocked. "A member of the Royal Canadian Mounted Police? Famous all over the world?"

"Well, lassie, I've lived my whole life in the wild. Sometimes society for a whole month is talking to a caribou. The loneliness seeps into you bones just like the rheumatism."

An old sourdough came dashing, bandy-legged, into the bar, waving nuggets to announce that he had hit it big and the drinks were on him.

Callie quickly got excited, but Claude put a damper on

it. "Harry Pigeon. He'll die broke. Already made and lost half a dozen fortunes."

"Any of them to you?" Mac asked.

"Oh, I unburdened him once over by Liarsville."

"You don't have to be so darned proud of it," Callie said.

"I'm not. That was one of the times when he was broke."

"If I don't get out there pretty soon, all the claims'll be spoken for. I don't see how sitting around in this saloon is going to help me."

"Hold your horses," Claude said. "You'll see."

It wasn't a long wait. At the next table: "You're a damned liar. That was the queen I give to you."

"You callin' me a liar, you cross-eyed anteater?"

Claude leaned over to butt in. "He did, I heard him." Turning his head to Mac, he said with a grin: "I told you."

"It was a jack. Jacka hearts, damn your eyes."

"I seen it plain. You was cheating on me, you ignorant whisky soak."

"Had it in his hat," Claude put in again.

"What are you doing?" Callie asked, grabbing his arm, appalled.

Claude smiled back pleasantly. "Getting you started."

Both gamblers threw back their chairs, alerting the whole room, and edged their hands toward their pistols.

It took something like that to galvanize the crowd; they began hitting the ground, tipping over tables and chairs, or running for the door.

Claude jumped to his feet and shouted: "The drop! The drop!"

It was immediately taken up by all the customers who remained, even those sprawled on their bellies. Fear and threats once again instantly transmuted into entertainment. The two would-be duelists relaxed slowly, moved their hands away from the pistols, and eventually allowed themselves to be fêted at the bar where the betting had already begun and their partisans would stand them drinks.

"What on earth's going on here?" Callie complained. "Why did you do that? That was a terrible thing to do, egging them on like that. They might have killed each other."

"Still might," Mac said dourly. "Claude has his ways."

Claude himself was not only unapologetic but slyly pleased with how things were going. "In a few minutes one of them isn't going to need his mining equipment."

Callie gripped her forehead. "Oh, Lord, no. Please, I don't want anyone hurt for me! What's the drop?"

Claude explained: "Two men race from the bar. Whoever gets through the door first can shoot the other. Anybody draws before they're through it gets strung up."

"That's barbaric!"

"That's rough justice," Claude said, grinning. "And it saves the furniture. Do it all the time up here."

"Only among heathens," Mac said. He suggested to Callie: "Too late to stop it now, lass, but you can close your eyes and put your head on my shoulder, if you want."

"I will not. I'm going to stop it."

She started to jump up, but both men reached out for an arm and yanked her none too gently back into her chair.

"Listen here, missy," Claude hissed in her ear, "try just once in your life not to have an opinion on something. We're not real popular around here, or haven't you noticed? And you can't change a whole territory, anyways."

She gave up, sitting back, but crossed her arms and set her jaw. "I will."

The bartender shouted—"Mush!"—and the two antagonists raced for the door amidst a huge roar of excitement.

Callie gave in and put her elbows on the table with her hands over her eyes, muttering about the evils of the Roman Colosseum.

The racers, having covered only thirty or forty feet, where bound to meet at the door where a vicious fight ensued. Kicking, biting, gouging, anything to get through first. Everyone moved close and crowded around so it was impossible to see from a table in the back, cheering first one battler and then the other according to who was on top at the moment.

Callie, eyes still covered, asked mordantly: "Don't you two want to witness the spectacle?"

"I've seen my share," Mac said.

A gruesome scream ushered from the fight scene, followed by another great roar of excitement; someone had broken through. And when the noise had subsided, a triumphant voice from somewhere out on the street. "I'm out! I'm out!" Then silence, followed by the same voice, less confident: "Where is he?"

Callic uncovered her eyes.

Now the voice was plaintive. "Send the bastard out here. Make him come out."

Another, stronger voice, a patron's: "Cain't. Leg's broke."

"Well . . . well . . . throw him out, god dammit."

"You're the one broke it, you damn' fool," someone else said, disgusted.

"It ain't fair."

"Aw, shut up."

"Come on in an' have a drink."

Everyone trudged back inside and up to the bar while a

couple lugged the injured man, groaning, to a large table in the corner, laid him there, and left him, his broken leg at an obtuse and very painful-looking angle.

"Sure doesn't look like that poor fella's going to the fields this year," Claude said. "Think I'll go over and buy him a bottle of Juice of the Snake. Better'n chloroform for pain."

The stable owner was a brawny man, so it was almost comical when he burst through the open door yelling hysterically: "The Swopes is comin'! Whole blessed clan! Thousands of 'em. Everybody come see."

They did, everyone in the place running for the door like a stampeded flock of chickens. Claude and Mac ambled after the throng. Callie, abandoned, wasn't going to be left behind. People pushed out onto the porch and even into the street to see the parade. At first everyone was jabbering, but as the lead wagons came into sight a hush fell over the group, over the whole town.

When Callie worked her way through to Mac, he said: "You wanted to know about the Swopes."

The caravan kept pouring in, a seemingly endless parade of ox-drawn freight wagons, moving slowly for effect. Many of the men accompanied on horse or mule back, although a dwarf and some children rode burros. The women were all on wagons, and a couple wore bandoleers of cartridges like brigands.

"I bet they're not even Christians," Callie said, watching the panorama of hard, sour faces drift past.

Claude said: "Not so's you notice."

"Strange how they brought their women and children," Callie said.

Mac explained: "They're jack Mormons from Utah. Run out of there by the church, they say. Drifting like Gypsies ever since."

"What do they want?"

"Everything you got," Claude said.

"And if that's all they take, I'd say you're pretty lucky," Mac told her.

Slocum appeared behind the trio. "Pretty sight?"

Callie sniffed at the air and wrinkled her face. "What's that odor?"

"Them," Claude said.

The Swopes resembled a separate species, unkempt, preternaturally ugly, heads and necks that tended to slope forward like wolves on the hunt, and a predisposition to scowl. Claude suggested that you might see them smile sometimes, but only if somebody was in pain.

Slocum said: "Time's coming, my friends, when miners' court's gonna look like the apex of civilization. By the way, Mister Emmett, you don't have to turn your face away from me. I believe I know who you are, and I'm not going to make any kind of fuss so long as you behave yourself around here."

Claude looked at him and showed a tiny slit of an utterly ambiguous smile—lethal, friendly, impossible to tell—but refrained from saying anything.

"He's leaving," Mac said.

Looking past them, Slocum said: "Here comes the old man."

If the people lining the streets were impressed before, they were awed by this to a near silence, made eerie by the creaking of the wagon wheels and braces and the grunting and clopping of beasts.

Everyone was looking at a tall, lean, black-suited patriarchal figure who resembled, deliberately, the John Brown of border children's nightmares. He sat his horse ramrod straight amongst a prætorian guard of his four heavily-armed sons, Jorem one of them.

Old man Swope simply raised his hand and the whole motley caravan came to a halt without comment. He rode over to a wagon and climbed aboard with an agility that belied his age. The four sons, putting their rifles akimbo to give the proceedings a certain bogus majesty, formed up in a square around their father. The latter stroked his full beard for a moment while his black eyes roamed the crowd.

"You all heerd of me. I'm John Brown Swope." His voice was deeply impressive and carried to the edges of the town. "And these here's my boys, McNab."

The oldest and steadiest-looking, like something out of the West.

"Tom."

He wore a stovepipe hat and a scarf, but it did nothing to disguise his genealogical debt to the higher apes. Spitting tobacco was perhaps an assertion of his humanness.

"Billy."

Fat with squeezed little eyes, seated on a too-small horse that had partially caved under him. He did smile, but it only served to demonstrate that he might be a little slow.

"And Jorem."

Jorem looked around slowly, apparently seeking someone.

"And this here is my family." His long arm swept the length and breadth of the horde. "They all come to help me bring some order to this benighted town. I've been appointed district judge by the governor of the territory, the Honorable Horace Rodgers." He pulled several sheaves of official-looking papers from inside his frock coat and waved them in the clear air.

"Want to ask to see 'em?" Slocum chuckled wickedly, addressing Claude.

"My McNab, here, he's to be marshal and the other boys'll be his deputies." Suddenly he smashed a fist into his other palm, making a sound like a gunshot. "Understand me, pilgrims! We bring the law of the Lord Jehovah here. You know your Book, or you ought to. A merciless law. Let no man or woman transgress it. Woe be unto them, justice will be swift and final."

"Reminds me of Papa," Callie whispered.

Whores began to leave the street in flocks, making the miners all the more glum and hangdog. One drunk tried to throw a bottle at John Brown Swope, but his friends quickly wrestled it away and thus saved his life.

Jorem, on a restless horse, finally spotted the trio—Slocum, too, had slipped away—and pantomimed someone being hung. Claude and Mac stared back, but the younger Swope only laughed.

"Time to go," Mac said.

"Past time," Claude agreed.

"We're not running away from these people, are we?" Callie asked.

"We sure as hell are," Claude said, getting a hold of her again and guiding her back into the saloon.

"Really," Callie insisted, "I'd rather be hung for a wolf than a sheep."

"You read that somewheres, didn't you," Claude said a little too patiently. He pulled down his shirt collar and tilted his head to reveal an angry red scar encircling the neck. "I been hung for a wolf, honey, and it ain't any improvement."

Chapter Ten

Within an hour of the Swopes' entrance, the trio slipped out of Daughton and were on the trail to the fields. Claude had given Callie the mule taken from the blue ticket. They were a little slow for his line of work.

Callie was unexpectedly sad. It had just struck her that she would never see either of these men again. The vastness swallowed friendships and lovers as easily as lives.

She tried hard to sound the opposite of what she was feeling. "Where you two going?"

"I thought," Mac said, "I'd just ride along with you up to the fields."

"Me, too," Claude said all too quickly.

"Oh, no. You two can ride anywhere you want, but I'm going mining by myself. I don't need your help."

The men rushed to say they believed her.

"I'm up here on a mission for people who sacrificed a lot to send me. They trust me to win through for them."

Mac insisted that he was going in that direction, anyway, and Claude said he also had business up there. Somewhere.

She let it drop.

"You were sent here on a family scout, boy. But you went and disobeyed my orders," John Brown Swope said to his son.

"No, I didn't, Daddy," Jorem pleaded in the high voice of a terrified ten-year-old. "I told you all was goin' on. I swear I did." He cowered, trying to keep some part of the stable between his father, a horsewhip in his hand and the equivalent in his eyes, and himself. Right now there was only a sawhorse with a saddle on it. Jorem tried to keep moving enough to stay out of reach, but not enough to inflame his father into acting. His three brothers crowded into the stable entrance, grinning, enjoying the show.

"You consorted with a low criminal name of King Otto. Two of you shot a miner in the camp up at Forty-Mile, and what did you get for it? You came here and got made a fool of. And it's that last I'm gonna take outta your hide."

"It ain't true, Daddy." He moved a little faster around the periphery of his father's rage. "Even if it was, when I got here, they used treachery on me. Who you gonna believe? I'm your own son."

"A disobedient son." John Brown lashed out quickly, and the tip of the whip caught Jorem's upraised arm.

The disobedient son cried out and moved a little faster, dodging and weaving; every instinct urged him to run away, but he didn't dare.

"Dance, little brother!" Tom called out cheerfully.

And McNab: "You can do better 'an that . . . I thought you liked dancin'."

"Try the Texas Two-Step, Jorem," Billy suggested, laughing so hard his sides hurt.

John Brown, with his long legs, began to take long steps, cutting off Jorem's room to maneuver. "A lazy, deceitful, blaspheming, disobedient son."

This time the whip cut into Jorem's cheek, a couple of inches from his right eye. He screamed this time from the pain, but he was also cognizant of how close he had come to being a one-eyed hellion. "Don't, Daddy! No! Please. . . ."

"Not my son, you're not. The Devil's spawn!" The old man at his work was a wonder, fast and quick as a mongoose. The whip struck again and again until Jorem's shirt and pants were ripped and the flesh bled from a dozen sizable cuts, until his screams were constant, one running right over another. His brothers loved it. Around town people locked their doors.

"Sic 'im, Daddy."

"Singe his britches."

"Caw! Caw! Caw!"

"Everybody's got a dream," Claude said a little defensively.

"All you want to do is steal from people," Callie pointed out.

"I got an ambition . . . same thing. Steal enough to open a bank." Claude looked at the other two, riding abreast with Callie in the middle, to find out how they were taking his declaration. "So people'd have a place to keep their money safe from people like me."

That did get a laugh, and Callie shook her head. "I never thought in my lifetime I'd ever hear people talk such things."

"I'd say that's a pretty fair stretch from your present occupation," Mac told him.

"I'm here to tell you how wrong you are, *Clarence*. Banking's the finest way to steal there is. Where I grew up in Oregon, bank stole the whole town. But when you do it that way, people tip their hats, give you first pick at the trough, and scheme for you to marry their daughters. James boys never had that kind of respect."

The trio got off and walked the horses when they entered the high country where the going was less sure and could be particularly wearing when on scree or talus. There was still plenty of light, and the views expanded forever in all directions on this crystalline spring afternoon. In the Far North, the descending sun reflected off a glacier and filled the sky with a premature pink haze.

The only smear on nature was Daughton, behind them, which looked like a metastasizing brown growth in the center of the burgeoning valley floor. Up here it was colder, too, making it necessary to pull up the collars on their coats, but the air was also redolent with alder and pine and fast-running water.

"Didn't you ever hear the Blue Parka Man called the Robin Hood of the North?"

Callie returned a flat—"No."—as they turned to follow the course of a small creek.

Mac gave it a horse laugh.

"I don't say everyone I robbed deserved it, but . . . you sure are hard on a man."

"What's this creek?" Callie asked. She pulled a map out of her coat pocket and tried to study it as she walked.

Mac said it was Fox Creek. "Wanders all over. Down where we met that first time, it's mostly called border creek."

"Matter of fact, it's the border up here, too," Claude put in.

Callie stopped her horse and mule. She surveyed the surrounding countryside, particularly behind her.

"Keep moving," Claude urged. "Got to find a campsite pretty soon." He took his own advice, mounted, and rode ahead.

"According to my map the border should be over there." She turned and pointed west.

"Miners and beavers build their dams, storms, landslides, and creeks are always changing course. Where'd you get that map?"

"The Putney Library."

"They're four, five thousand miles from here," Mac said, unbelieving.

"I don't care. I should think if it was something as important as a border between two countries you'd want. . . ."

"I'm the border," Mac grumped, and tramped ahead to get away from her.

Sometimes, Callie was learning, men were just babies with big parts.

The fire glowed back at them from facets of the surrounding rocks and their own eyes as with resting cats. Callie reached up to feel the warmth in her face and knew that, while some of the heat issued from the pile of burning cones and branches, the rest was instigated by simple joy. She studied the two tired men opposite through the steam from her coffee cup and wondered how they could allow themselves to get tired when all of this was so glorious.

"The old gentleman was in the Mounted Police before me. Actually I was born in Scotland but raised here, in a cabin just like the one I've got now. God-forsaken place. Only that one, at least, was graced by a woman's presence. Would have been unbearable without my mother."

Mac looked deliberately at Callie with a long, serious face; out of self-consciousness she brought up a smile, but then couldn't prevent it freezing. Yet when he turned away and went on, staring into the fire, it was matter-of-factly, without any trace of self-pity.

"Poor Mother was a city girl all the way. I think it killed her in the end. Kills a lot of women, or drives them mad. I was about ten . . . more or less. You lose track in the wild."

"That's so sad," Callie said.

Mac seemed surprised. "Is it? It's a life no different than many up here. We choose it."

"Well, Miss Callie, it's your turn," Claude said.

"What?"

"Tell us about *your* life."

She smiled to herself. "It's just beginning."

Mac checked the stars and decided, never mind the amount of light still, it was time for them to sleep. "Make the fields midday if we're lucky."

Everyone stood and stretched. Callie pointed at the rocks to the north. "I'm going that way."

The men each picked their spot at roughly a hundred and twenty degrees opposite, and everyone headed off into the bush. In Callie's case, it was well into the boulders, bluffs, and trees where the light barely penetrated. Tramping uphill, stumbling, cold, finally she found some shelter that definitely settled the question of privacy and lowered her pants and bloomers.

It was the act of squatting and arranging herself that took her eyes skyward, not far, not at the Pleiades or Ursa Minor, just to the top of the stack of rocks directly in front of her . . . where a stark, apparitional figure stood as unmoving as the stone itself, staring down at her. Her scream carried across plains, mountains, and glaciers, frightening feral beasts into their holes and birds into the safety of the skies.

Chapter Eleven

Callie started running before she got her pants up and got only a few steps, those in midair, before taking a resounding tumble, rolling on the rocky ground. Through sheer will she was up and running without ever pausing in her forward motion, yanking all the harder at a flapping belt.

When she reached the campsite, she literally ran bang into Claude, while Mac nearly ran into the two of them. Both men, like the worst farce, with galluses flying behind, holding up their own pants, but with guns in their free hands.

"Someone . . . up on the . . . rocks," she barely got out, panting.

The men dashed off in the direction she had indicated. Callie finally took the time to secure her pants and hurried after them, unwilling to be left alone.

Mac saw the figure first—"There!"—and ducked for the cover of a tree. Claude crowded in behind him.

"Who are you?" the Mountie called out. "Speak up or I'll fire."

"Sergeant MacDonald?"

"Oh, my Lord," Mac said, grinning. He relaxed and told Claude—"You can put your pistol back."—then called up to the still unmoving figure: "Hello, Skookum!"

"You know him?" Callie, coming to join, demanded querulously.

"Su-ure. Skookum Jim. He's an old buddy, scouts for us."

"What's he doing creeping around our camp?" Claude asked.

"Jim doesn't creep, he just comes unexpected. How's he know there's not a dangerous trail robber down here?"

Claude would have snapped back, but Callie, still annoyed, butted in: "You certainly have some peculiar friends, Sergeant. He gave me the fright of my life, standing up there so still. He could have been after anything."

Mac tried to reassure her: "This isn't the Wild West, Miss Fisk. Our Indians up here are good citizens, unless they're drunk, which pretty much goes for everybody."

"You'll get used to these things," Claude said.

Callie liked being patronized least of all. She stomped back to the camp, embarrassed, pouting a little.

"Come on in and get warm, Skookum, have a cuppa!" Mac shouted.

Callie sat on her haunches by the campfire but never quite settled in, looking as if she might bolt at any moment despite the fact that she was confronting a sixty-year-old Indian smoking a cigar, wearing a derby, and suffering a bad cold.

What brought her around to the men's conversation were the words: "You come back Canada, Sergeant. Trouble, maybe big."

"I'll get there, Skookum. I been over in Daughton for a couple days on official business." He avoided looking at his companions when he said that.

"War could happen, you don' come back now. Chief Charley of Charley River Tribe say Eagle Jack steal dog of his."

Mac sagged a little and rubbed his eyes with an air of resignation.

"I can see her through the night," Claude persisted,

"and get her there midday tomorrow, so there's really nothing keeping you here." He smiled, but no one was fooled.

"Really, Sergeant, a war over a dog?"

"No, miss, Skookum's right. I've got to go back."

"Not tonight, surely! Isn't there . . . well, couldn't Mister Emmett give Skookum enough from his ill-gotten gains for a new dog?"

"Generous of you," Claude said sourly.

"No, lass, he can't. It's honor. Mine as well as theirs." He stood and told Skookum he would collect his things.

As he went about packing and loading his horse, Callie, frustrated, turned on Claude: "Can't you do anything except make smart-alecky remarks? Talk to him."

"Why?"

"He's a lonely man who enjoys our company."

Claude managed, with effort, to look as solemn as a deacon. "You don't get between a man and his job."

"How would you know?"

"Oh, that's unfair. I have my profession. You just don't approve of it with that New England Puritan nose-in-the air of yours. Mind you, it's not a bad nose. In fact. . . ."

"I don't find you at all amusing, just . . . ridiculous." She marched over to where the Mountie was already cinching up his pack.

"Mac, surely someone else could settle a silly little dispute like this."

He turned on her with a sternness and heat in his eyes that was for the second time unexpected. "Mind your manners, Miss Fisk." He glanced at the Indian to see if he had heard. "It's not silly. You haven't been here long enough to say that."

Callie stammered: "I . . . I'm sorry. I didn't realize. . . ."

"I told you!" Claude called over.

"Oh, be quiet!" She started back to him, but was jarred to a dramatic halt by Mac's large hand gripping one shoulder, almost to the point of pain.

"Miss Fisk, please?"

When Callie turned to find him so close, she could feel his warm breath in the chilly night air; her eyes were jacked wide open. "Oh!"

"Callie." He addressed her as if it took enormous audacity on his part. "I'm sorry for being short with you." He paused again but hung on. "Come with me," he blurted.

"What?"

"Come with me. To Dawson."

"Oh, my goodness. Sergeant! Whatever are you sug. . . ."

"No, no, please. Don't misunderstand me. I meant for a proper Mountie wedding." He spoke so rapidly it made him breathless. "Under crossed swords? You'd like that, wouldn't you? With the commandant and his lady and the whole regiment looking on."

Struggling with her own incredulity, she heard Claude, back by the fire, laugh in such a way that it could have been the mule. It made her angry, and consequently more tolerant of MacDonald's mad importunity.

"Mac, we just met."

"Up here people marry before they've met."

"I'm not one of them. It's impossible!"

"Callie, I've been in love with you since that first time I didn't shoot you."

Claude came ambling over, clearly up to no good. "What kind of life you offering her, MacDonald?"

"One with a man she can depend on. Loyalty, dependability, safety, things you know nothing about."

Claude yawned a little theatrically.

It was not lost on Mac, who drew himself up like a buck in season, instantly throwing off his fatigue. "And what would you offer, a low man like you?"

"Me?" Claude's eyes actually bore a flash of, at the least, confusion. "I'm not saying I'm offering anything. But if I did, you can be sure it'd be a world of fine things, not a shack in the wilderness. A high time in places she's never been, adventures. . . ."

"As the wife . . . if you intend *marrying* her . . . of a bushwhacker and trail robber? Always sneaking and hiding and lying? And what happens to her when you go up the long ladder and down the short rope, I'd like to know. Have you thought of that?"

"Better than being bored to death at an early age, you brass-button, tight-assed son-of-a-bitch."

Mac, really inflamed now, turned to Callie in outrage. "There! Did you hear that? Doesn't even know how to talk to a decent woman." He growled at Claude: "You say one more blue word in front of this young lady. . . ."

Callie was transfixed; this was truly wonderful! Two men, two handsome, strong men fighting over her. Was that possible? It was before her eyes but still incredible.

"Why do you think she wants *me* to stay?" Mac demanded to know. "Protection from you, laddie."

"Why's she need protection from me? I saved her life."

"So did I."

"I saved it twice."

"That's not the kind of protection I meant."

No woman in Bent Creek, even Betty Anne Blodget of the golden hair and silver breasts, had ever had a tribute from the opposite sex of such epic grandeur. This was worth all the horrible things she had experienced since she had come to the Yukon.

"Why wouldn't she be safer with me, when I'm the best pistol shot in the territory?"

"You might just have to prove that, bucko."

For one terrible moment she wondered: *What if they actually had a duel, shot it out over me and one was killed? Over me! Like in a novel, Count Tolstoy. Gloria!*

Raised voices, angry voices on the point of violent confrontation, broke through into the fantasy and caused it to be flung off like a bridal gown on the wedding night. What were these monstrous thoughts? She rushed over to grab up the old shotgun from next to her bedroll, shouted—"Stop this, you two!"—and fired one barrel into the air.

Claude shouted—"Run for cover!"—to the friend he had been about to kill, and the both of them ducked low for the nearest tree. Callie remained standing in the middle of the clearing, holding the smoking gun with a defiant look on her face. The men shouted for her to get under something.

"You want to stop doing that," Claude said, shaking his head. But the enmity was over.

"You listen to me now, you two. I'm taking a stand. I'm real flattered, and I like you both very much, but I came here on a mission, and I don't intend to take up with anybody. Is that clear? We're just friends. I'm sorry, Mac."

The vinegar had gone out of both of them, bringing them slowly to the ground in the posture of two collapsed bags of escaping air.

Approaching midday, moving silently abreast on a trail through a sweet-smelling pine forest, Callie looked aside and studied Claude. "You weren't going in this direction, were you?"

He was very casual. "I got some business to conduct up near Lousetown."

"Surely not prospecting?"

"Hell, no. Only fools do that."

"Thank you very much."

"Don't say I didn't tell you."

"You're always telling me something I don't want to hear."

"There's still a few things you don't know." They rode for a few minutes in silence. "One of them's right over that next ridge up there."

When they topped the crest, a vast landscape spread out to either side, bisected almost perfectly by a river gushing out of a gap in the hills directly below.

"Caribou River," Claude said.

Wide, shallow, and fast-running. A fascinating sight, made even more so by the hundreds—it seemed thousands—of miners and their camps stretched out along both banks as far as the eye could discern. The distance between them measured in yards.

Callie didn't want to, but she gasped: "Oh, my sweet Aunt Emma." She climbed down off of her horse, as if she needed solid ground beneath her feet.

Claude followed, politely keeping any smugness to himself.

"That's the most discouraging sight I ever witnessed," Callie said.

"Gold washes out of that cut below us, down from the mountains. Gets caught up in all the gravel and rocks. So farther out you go, less chance you got of finding anything. Try to horn in at this end and they'll kill you without a thought to your being a woman." He waited again.

Callie considered this for a moment and then put resolution into her posture. "If it's that hard, I guess I better get started."

"You'll likely be the only female down there."

"Good. Then they'll underrate me."

Tuning out for a moment, concentrating on the problems confronting her, Callie was brought up short by catching some of what Claude was saying: ". . . I'm going another way from here on, so you won't have to concern yourself about my morals, Miss Fisk. We all pay sooner or later, don't we? One way or the other." What else had he said? The sadness surprised and unsettled her.

They shook hands. Her mind was a blur. He mounted and rode off down a side trail without looking back.

When Callie pulled herself together, she knew what she had to say to him and shouted it down at his disappearing form. "I'll see you again! I'll see everybody! And I'll've done my job and be rich because I'm no slacker!"

Callie found the miners less hostile than she had anticipated, but, on the other hand, not particularly helpful. Their main concern was that she not set up camp close by. The distances between different stakes followed a general pattern of around a hundred feet or so, and once established in the prospector's mind were zealously guarded. One trespassed anywhere at the peril of one's life.

As she moved along the river toward its unclear end, looking for the place no one else wanted, she was a keen observer. Often the excuse for stopping by a moment, always asking permission, was to tell the isolated and information-starved miners, almost all of them cheechakos like herself, tales of recent events in the great outside. Sometimes she crossed her fingers and told white lies if it would ease their loneliness.

Within a couple of days she had her camp established and had begun construction on a primitive sluice, using an illustration in her library book for a design plan. Hours every day were allotted to wading around panning. The icy water rushing to batter against her legs, hands, and hips, stinging them blue and paralyzed, so that she had to come out every few minutes, restore the circulation and feeling, then stomp back in to begin the cycle of pain and numbness all over again

At night she sat hunched over the fire with the loaded shotgun close beside her and tried to massage her own hurting back, amazed at how quickly her small cache of food and drink withered in the wild. Still, Callie was capable of hard work and endurance beyond that of many of the young men drawn here from the cities of the world. *I suppose,* she would think in her aching misery, *I owe that to Papa.* She did work hard, all day every day.

And it was observed. She felt it but could never quite confirm her instincts; once at twilight she thought she saw a stooped figure on a rock high above her, but the onrushing dark of a thunderhead took its definition away in a swallow. What could anyone possibly want from her? In several days she had failed to find a single speck of gold dust in the turbulent water. On that score, there was nothing to do but go on, albeit with diminishing hopes.

Chapter Twelve

With painfully frozen fingers, Callie picked through the gravel in the pan, shook it hard through the sieve, and picked some more. She had gotten into the habit of straining to see what she wanted to see among the millions of minute particles, and it was taking a toll on her eyes. Now they competed with the rest of her body parts to see which could inflict the most discomfort.

What with the coming of warmer weather, black flies and mosquitoes had come to haunt her nights with bites and their interminable buzzings that were worse than the itching. There was no relief from them.

Once a man on the other bank had exposed himself to her, dancing around and waving his willie in the wind on a chilly day, shouting unbelievable obscenities, so that in the end she had to get the shotgun to discourage him. She put it down to his being mad—lots of people up here went mad, they said. She had seen rams, stallions, and bulls when tumescent—thank God his didn't look like that.

Other miners within distant view had answered the call to nature without an excess of precaution, and she would have to turn away quickly and pretend. Since there was nothing mad in that, perhaps in the day-to-day struggle they had simply forgotten that she was present. Thank God, Mac and Claude, tough as they were, showed far more gentility, otherwise she might have become disenchanted with the whole male sex.

Hardship, rain, pain, and lack of success were not

enough; her period came on, something for which she had neglected to prepare, at least out here. Her bar of soap was wearing thin, and there was a definite shortage of rags, although plenty of water. She would have to restrict herself to working ankle-deep along the banks.

One morning she woke up late because she had a slight fever and it was overcast—normally the sun awakened her—dressed, and went outside to confront a strange presence. Directly across the river was a party of mounted men dressed, on the whole, in khaki with a couple of Indians. Some had round hats, some fur, or woolen caps with ear flaps against the morning chill. Several mules carried an assortment of surveying devices.

For a few moments the two sides simply regarded each other across the water. The men seem confused, possibly about her sex. Finally the officer in front nodded and waved.

Callie cupped her hands and called over: "Who are you?"

He hollered back: "Lieutenant A. J. Cross, ma'am, Twenty-First Battalion, U.S. Army Engineers Survey Team. Drawing up new maps of the territory."

"Listen! If I had a question about boundaries, would you help me?"

"Sure thing, ma'am, How we gonna get together?"

Callie didn't hesitate, period be darned; she leaped into the water and plunged across, kicking up huge plumes of spray. The troopers whooped and cheered encouragement.

In the second week she went as far as the foothills on her side of the valley and bagged a rabbit. The old shotgun shredded it, but she stripped, cleaned, and cooked the shreds. What she didn't eat right away was put in the sun to dry. A few days later she shot a goose, but only because it had been brought to earth by an injured wing. She felt badly about that, but in the long run was too hungry to care.

It was easing into high summer, and there were wildflowers and green vegetation everywhere to compensate for the insects. But it also meant predators; on three occasions she had seen bears. They could put a large hole in your day if they hung around. When she spotted a grizzly, she couldn't bring herself to do anything but sit in the entrance to her tent—not that she thought canvas could protect her from those giant claws—with her shotgun cradled, and keep it in view as long as it was in the neighborhood.

On top of her other troubles, there was still the occasional appearance of phantom figures in the rocks and on the hills above her. Some mounted, some not, seen most often against the dawn or in the gray light of evening. Some she felt were watching, others passing. Sunlight glinted off the lens's of telescopes.

She couldn't sleep the night of the grizzly and was up early and hard at work. *Root little hog or die,* she told herself; things were closing in. And then an hour into exploring the river bottom, she found something in her pan, a sizable nugget. She had to resist a cheer, but did jump up and down, splashing herself wet and cold before remembering how it was not healthy to advertise success in the fields.

As she tried to run, plowing through thigh-high water to the bank, an old man's voice startled her: "What you thunk you got?"

He had come up from behind a boulder on the other side of the river without her having the slightest inkling of his presence. Now he sat atop it. Old and bent, puffing on a pipe, and seemingly unarmed, all that reassured her a little.

Still, she called back: "None of your business!" She had heard the tales.

"You a boy or a girl?"

She stood on her bank, drying off, and looked across at him. He did have a nice old Santa Claus smile, and she was desperate for human contact. The question was impertinent, though, so she answered in the same manner: "What do I look like?"

"A boy."

"Have it your way."

"You're strong and a hard worker, but you ain't never gonna find no gold way up here on this no-'count river. All panned out."

Callie had placed her own pan on the ground, but now she bent over and slowly raised the nugget into the pristine morning air, milking her triumph. "Oh? And what about that, sir?" She even let out a little whoop. "There's gold. Right here this morning."

"I know. I been watchin' you." He slid down off the boulder and started across the river, staggering against the current to the point where Callie called a halt in her triumph, holding her breath for a moment, prepared to plunge in if she had to. She even reached out her hand to help haul him in when he reached her side. He was cold and winded but smiling through his bushy gray beard

"Thankee. I'm called Wild-Water Ned by the way . . . don't 'member my real name no more. Let's see your gold."

Callie showed it without hesitation now. "What do you think of that?"

He shook his head, and a lot of tangled, unwashed gray hair quivered. "Not much," he said in a voice that cracked so often it made everything he said sound like a cackle. "It's iron pyrites." Then, a little too pointedly for Callie's liking, he added: "Fool's gold."

Callie believed him, groaned, and sagged right down to the ground.

"I'd get down there with you, but I'd likely never get up. Don't feel too bad, ever' cheechako makes that mistake least once."

She sunk her head in her hands. "You don't understand. It isn't just this. . . . Go away so I can cry."

"You're a girl."

"I know."

"No bother, you're still aces for what I need. See, like I say, I been watchin' you real good, an' I got a proposition to make."

She stiffened a little and looked up at him. "What are you talking about?"

"These boys up and down here, this creek, they're just cattle. Foller one another. Packa fools, got their snouts so far down in the trough they can't see the banquet life's settin' out for 'em. Now me, I got a better idea." He pointed to the other side of the river. "In them hills there's a place where a river use' t' come down. Wouldn't be surprised if it was back when there was dinosaurs. Mighty promisin' . . . I got some nuggets already." He reached into his pocket and extracted one.

Callie was impressed but didn't want to show it. "How do I know that isn't fool's gold?"

"It ain't, miss, it ain't. After you been here a spell, you'll know the difference." If nothing else, the glow in his own eyes would have been hard to fake.

"All right. But what do you need me for?"

The old man cackled again. "Strong back. It takes diggin', not like here. 'Sides, I can trust a woman."

"How do you know that? You ever hear of Lucretia Borgia? There have been some famous women who were evil."

He snickered this time. "You ain't one of 'em. I told you, I been watchin' you."

"You didn't even know if I was a boy or a girl."

"I know'd what was important."

He had such a shrewd look she believed him. "Why should I trust *you?*"

"Hellfire, look at me, girl. I'm too old to be mean or bad. I'm canny, I don't deny that, but I'm jist awful old. Name's Wild-Water Ned, by the way. Don't 'member my real name." He reached out to shake her hand.

She reminded him—"You told me."—but took it anyway. "How did you get called Wild-Water?"

"I fergit that, too. Musta been a reason. See what I mean? I'm harmless."

"Mister Ned, I'm young and maybe I'm still stupid about a lot of things, but something I have learned since I came up here to Alaska is never trust anyone who tells you they're old and harmless, never trust anyone who asks you to trust them, and, in fact, if I let myself, never trust anyone. I know that's not right, but I'm just trying to get along."

The old man wasn't insulted; in fact, he was already whooping with phlegmish laughter before she even finished, and by the time she did he was up and performing a little hand-clapping jig on the bank with the river lapping at his boots. "I knew I picked right! Hot damn, I knew it!" he crowed, singing it.

Callie refused to be impressed by all this unrestrained enthusiasm for her. "There's probably some other reason besides a strong back and an honest face, isn't there?"

"Sure 'nuff. Claim jumpers, bears, wolves, evil spirits, too, in them hills. Man's gotta sleep sometime, and that's when they git you. Two can guard a claim real good. One's no good, at all. See . . . look up on that ridge over there." He pointed over his shoulder in the direction he had indicated previously.

"I don't see anything."

"Keep lookin'. You will."

There was a vaporous mist that came over the hills every midday when the sun brought the deep frost to the surface as moisture. It was not dense enough to hide anything but created distortion that required extra effort from an observer. Gradually Callie began to make out a figure on the ridgeline that dominated the range.

"Not very well . . . but I see something."

"I tell you, there's an evil wind comin'. My arthur-itis feels it jist like an act of nature. Talk is all along the creek a-bein' spied on, someone wantin' their gold, somebody big, they say, too big to fight. Ever'body jist wants to git their haul and haul outta here. Now, over there . . ."—he pointed to where he prospected—"we'd likely be safe from it for a while. Whatta ya say . . . pardners?"

Callie glanced at the ghost rider, thought she saw the sun glint on a bit of glass, and wondered if he wasn't watching them in return. It made up her mind for her; she turned back to Ned, smiled, and stuck out her hand. "Partners."

"Don't fergit to bring that big scatter-gun, will you?"

"Callie Fisk."

"Wild-Water Ned. Don't 'member my. . . ."

Chapter Thirteen

A hard rain falling. Two days now. The close proximity of the tall pines to three sides of the cabin protected it somewhat, but the damp was not fooled, nor were the insects. It was almost warm, and, if a mosquito can sound happy, the ones buzzing around Mac's head, as he sat in his open doorway looking out, were ecstatic. He let them bite him, his skin inured to the surprise. This way they wouldn't bother to go inside and disturb his sleep.

The Indian housekeeper had left to visit her family and not returned. Things like that happened up here.

He sat in his trail pants, galluses, and the top of his long johns with a blanket draped over his shoulders against the damp, smoking his meerschaum. It, too, tasted damp and sour today. The only reading available was his mother's Presbyterian Bible and Bobbie Burns's "Tam o'Shanter" that he saved for winter, the former for its solace and the latter for its humor.

He took out his wallet and extracted a dog-eared photograph, already turning brown. It was the one taken of the three of them on that sunny, hopeful morning in Dogtown, a moment caught out of time in what now seemed like another century. He could only allow himself an occasional look; like everything else up here it had to be rationed, and it wasn't due for viewing until Saturday. The rain had driven him to it. Carefully he put it back.

After a while, for lack of anything else, he sang softly under his breath to the rain.

Cheeks as bright as rowans are
Brighter far than any star
Fairest of them all by far
Is my darlin' Callll-lie Mairi. . . .

He was proud of his baritone, but even if he was deluded, so what, there was no one to hear him. No one. No one. . . .

Ned was right; it asked for a strong back. Callie's. There was no ignoring that his own was decrepit. She accepted that; she didn't really mind doing most of the hard work. In fact, after all the discouragement of the last weeks, it felt good just to be involved in something that offered at least a smidgen of hope.

When you looked at old Wild-Water, you had to grin, forty, fifty years minimally at dreaming, hoping, and losing, and he was still an optimist. She liked her new companion; it was reassuring to know that you could be as old as Papa without having to be Papa. He told wonderful tales to liven dinner around the fire, stories that were sometimes very fanciful yet wonderful.

One night a pack of wolves came close to the fire. Their red eyes, glaring out of the dark, frightened Callie, but Ned insisted they were not a threat unless you were on your way to being carrion. He threw a firebrand out into the rocks to prove his point, and, sure enough, they scattered, sounding intimidated.

Callie was able to look down and see the camps along the river. Ned could just make out their fires at night. After a few days, she noticed that they were fewer; some campfires were definitely extinguished. Like the young in every species, she was curious and wanted to go down to find out the reason.

"You jist keep on diggin' like you promised me you'd do." It wasn't as if Ned was lazy; he had done his share and more, and she *had* promised. "None of our beeswax what them poor fools do down there. Trouble's comin' for 'em, and you don't wanna lead it right back up here."

This particular "gold train," as it was called locally, approached the modest in appearance in that it was only four mules laden with canvas sacks of dust and nuggets, accompanied by four guards whose primeval appearance mocked the pretensions of nature. One on horseback and the other three plodding along beside. A wolf pack, upon sighting this bunch, would have fled into the deep forest.

However small it appeared at first glance, monetarily their load was worth almost a hundred thousand dollars back in civilization. Enough to set any normal man up for life.

The rider, Red Rhuel, wore yellow boots and a feather in his cap. His scarred face was barely perceptible through a jungle of matted vines that passed for hair. None of them spoke much, as they were in the high hill country where going was rough. Conversation was one of their lesser pleasures under the best of conditions.

They came around a corner in the trail, and Red perceived something ahead that caused him to rein in. The men behind him may have appeared sloppy, but they knew what they were about and what they were carrying. Not to mention the price of failure. Within seconds, everyone had a gun out and was looking around for something to shoot. Those were their orders: "Anyone gets too close 'tween here and the coast, shoot on sight."

"Whoa! Lookie there!" Red exclaimed, climbing down from his horse, indicating something posed on a rock beside the trail. The others gathered around him, squinting.

They speculated as to what he was pointing at, but Red could see it clearly. About a hundred feet ahead, it was a bottle of brandy with a ribbon around it and some kind of note attached, summoning the weak and thirsty with all the subtlety of a two-dollar whore.

"Whatta ya think of that, huh, boys?"

One guard, a huge man as big as the mules, said: "I think we got us a little luck fer a change."

"I never had that kinda luck afore," another one said. "Sump'in's peculiar. I better just shoot it."

Red slapped his rifle away. "Hell you will, you dumb ox." He remounted. "My mama's son don't pass on no gift horses."

The nay-sayer, a wiry little man with one eye, still wasn't satisfied. "I wouldn't touch it, Red."

Red did, riding forward and leaning low in the saddle to reach down and to scoop it up. "This here's brandy from France. I never had none of this in my whole life."

"Ol' John Brown Swope'll skin us alive," the one-eyed one pleaded.

"What's the writin' on it?" the fourth one asked.

Red worked at it. "My daddy . . . was . . . saved . . . from freezin' . . . here. God . . . tol' me to do sump'in good. May this help . . . you . . . like it done him."

He yanked the already loosened cork out of the bottle and, holding it to the sky like an offering, took a huge swig that was followed the instant the bottle left his mouth by a hillbilly war cry. "Holy sheeeit, that's good!" He moved back to the group, holding out his trophy in one hand.

The woolly mammoth told the others in his deeper-than-bass, rumbling voice that sounded like God's: "It's like a church offerin'. Lord's sayin' it's the right thing to do." He reached to catch the bottle as it came close and get it to his own lips in one sweeping move.

The others watched, saw, as if through glass tubing, the animal satisfaction radiate his entire body. After several swallows they grew alarmed, began to yell that he was drinking too much, and threatened to shoot him if he didn't give it over. Even little one-eye fought for the right to have the next swill.

"Whoooeee!" the big man said, coughing pleasurably. "Man'd go to Hades in a hand basket for that."

They passed it around . . . and around . . . and. . . .

Callie sat beside her tent, studying an ore sample. She had just brought a sack of dirt and shale down the hill to the sorting area. Outside of some chipper birds, the occasional clang of Ned's pickaxe, and a slight breeze rustling the trees and shrubs, it was very quiet, a state that Callie had grown used to and found blissful.

Her partner continued to insist that he do some of the work. She understood that allowing him some exercise was a necessary trade-off on male pride, even old male pride. She appreciated his cranky insistence on independence even if sometimes it was irrational.

There was cry from above that caused her to drop the sample and look to the mine. Not that she could see it from where she sat; there was foliage and an outcropping in the way. She jumped up and began to run, then had to run back for the shotgun. It had to be cracked open on the way to see if it was loaded. The cries continued, growing louder, but it was impossible to make out their tenor because all of Ned's sounds, no matter how high-pitched, were gravelly, inarticulate.

Yelling to him as she scrambled upward: "Ned! Where

are you? What's happened?" She found him out on the terrace where they had dug into the hill—dancing, holding up a piece of rock, his pickaxe and shovel at his feet.

"Callie! Gold! We struck it, honey. A whole vein, a couple feet from the surface, goin' and goin' an' wide as my chest."

Callie stopped, struck uncharacteristically speechless for a moment. Ned didn't even notice; he couldn't take his eyes off the nugget that he held out in front of him as he danced around.

"Are you sure?" she asked feebly.

"Wouldn't I know after all these years." He slowed to a little footwork in place, catching his wind. "An' we only jist dug a dent in that hill. You're my luck, sweetheart."

She reached out for the nugget, but he thought she wanted to dance, so grabbed her hand instead and began to swing her around, singing madly to accompany his feet.

Buffalo gal, won't you come out tonight?
Come out tonight?
Come out tonight. . . .

At first Callie was so surprised it was all she could do to keep her balance, but ecstasy in an old man is a rare sight in this life, one that isn't resisted for long. First she threw her head back and laughed extravagantly, something rare enough in her life, then joined in the singing.

Buffalo gal, won't you come out tonight?
And dance by the light of the moon?

They continued their manic tour around the border of sanity while the sounds of joy bounced back from the woods and hills on all sides and enveloped them.

Buffalo gal. . . .

Along with something else—horses' hoofs clopping and slipping on rocks and shale just below. She heard it first and stopped them abruptly. Ned's hearing wasn't as keen, but there was nothing wrong with his instincts; he went on point with his head up.

She broke away and did some tumbling and sliding herself on the way down to where she thought the sounds originated. Ned had misplaced his old pistol and scrambled around looking for it.

Callie ran out across the hill, and then through some trees. She hoped to see the visitor first, but he saw her. It didn't matter; this was a scarecrow of a man on a poor-looking horse, ragged, dust-covered black clothes, no sign of a weapon. Riding with his feet and elbows akimbo, he reminded her of Ichabod Crane in the story. His direction was uphill, out of the valley, making it all too apparent he was in flight.

Nevertheless, she made certain that the shotgun showed large when she hailed him.

"Hey, hey, you there, boy!" he called back, the fear that had driven him this far marking every feature.

Callie didn't think it worth correcting him. She started to say something, but he was playing Paul Revere, and Revere was not a listener.

"You got any sense, boy, you'll get out. Fast." With that he looked away from her and concentrated on the way ahead, since he was making his own rough trail.

"What are you running from?"

"Marauders! Fiends from hell! Killin' people . . . kilt my partner . . . !"

"Who are they?" she shouted back.

"I tolt you." He speeded up, urging his horse into a copse of trees, afraid, apparently, even of her, and disappeared.

She went up and gave Ned the message. He shrugged it off—nothing short of the planet crumbling was capable of undermining the resplendent joy of a real strike.

"Fancy 'nother dance, partner?"

The bottle lay on its side in the clearing, more than empty—sucked dry. The ants crawling over and into it seemed in the grip of a furious curiosity but hadn't a hope of a big night. The men who had accomplished this miraculous evacuation lay around, too, helpless but dreaming in such a way as to be indifferent to their state. Next to Red were his yellow boots, yanked off at the last minute as the crushing languor overcame him, set down neatly, side by side. Of the four, he was the one closest to consciousness and that was relative.

Flat on his back, unable even to turn over, he did find the capability to raise his head a little and rest it on a rock. There was a blue mushroom approaching. It swam from side to side, jiggled around in front of him, and even changed color several times. A not unpleasant dream if somewhat addled.

The mushroom seemed to issue a command: "Stand and deliver!" Talking plants now? Someone laughed, and Red laughed with him.

Red thought he heard one of his pack mutter faintly: "Blue Parka Man." If it was true, the fact of a known terror, the Blue Parka Man, was somehow reassuring. It even seemed to clear his vision a bit. "Wha' was in 'at . . . damn' . . . hooch?" he managed with a thick and absent tongue.

"Laudanum," Claude said, his voice muffled by the bandanna over his face. He was going around collecting the mules bearing the gold, and examining the contents of two sacks. "You boys'll have sweet dreams and peaceful bowels for some time to come."

He started the mules off, all strung together, patting the gold pouches as they passed by. What he should have done was looked closely at the tiny stencil on the bottom right-hand corner of each sack, a representation of the compass of the Master Architect of the universe, but he was having too much fun.

Removing the saddle from Red's horse, it was set loose to make its own way. Next their weapons were sent flying into a nearby ravine where at the very least it would require a good long, strenuous effort to recover them.

When Claude showed signs of leaving, Red managed to speak again in his dreamy whisper: "That there's . . . Swope . . . gold."

"I'll wash it good." Claude strolled away in the direction the mules had presciently taken, humming contentedly to himself.

"Lemme figure now." The blanket was filled with nuggets, some still embedded and layered with packed dirt. The fire made them light gloriously, big healthy fireflies dancing in the imagination.

Maybe . . . seven, eight thousand, more or less."

Callie was thrilled. "Four thousand apiece."

"Jist the beginnin'."

She gave a yell of pleasure and rocked back where she was sitting on the ground. "I can't believe it."

"Now'd be a fair time to start. It's an awful rich strike, kind I been lookin' for all my life."

"It's wonderful. I can give the church back a thousand right now. Then, if I can figure a way to sneak it past Papa, I could give a thousand to Mama. If my little sister wanted to go to college, I could put a thousand aside for that."

"What you aimin' to do for yourself?"

She looked off across the valley, not with trepidation but still as if the whole world hidden out there in the dark was unknown. "I don't know. What'll you do with yours?"

"Oh, probably set to work seein' how fast I can throw it away. You know, whisky, women, and song, if you'll fergive my language. See, I got to, 'cause I got to have some reason to come right back to look for more. It's all I ever done I liked, honey. I'm jist an old sourdough, an' I 'spect I'll die where the wolves'll pick my bones clean."

"Oh, Ned, that sounds so . . . hopeless."

"That's you bein' young speakin'. I don't see nothin' bad in it."

Callie drooped, looking a little depressed for someone who had just made four thousand dollars. "At least you know what you want."

Claude had taken the gold up to his hiding place in the hills. A lot of time and effort went into concealing it and his access to it. Two whole days of digging, trampling, sweeping, dragging. He had not lived this long being careless. When he was through, he took the mules down near Lousetown and released them. Finders keepers.

The night he finished, sitting by his campfire in the shelter of some rocks, Claude felt an inexplicable emptiness. He was rich. That's what he had come here for, to this cruel country. What else did he want from it? From life? He tried singing to drive off the devils of thought.

Oh, we never speak of Aunt Clara,
her picture is turned to the wall.
Though she lives on the French Riviera,
Mother says she is lost to us alllll. . . .

First the wolves and then silence drowned him out. There wasn't enough light to read, and he was too tired to build up the fire. Too tired to sleep. He did what thousands of lonely campers have done, and rummaged though his pack for a picture. Usually it was of a girl friend or family, but he didn't really have the former, and the latter had rightly turned him out. No, it would have to be of himself with his two unlikely companions, since it was the only one he had. Come to think of it, they were the only two *friends* he had.

Callie! Oh, my God, that couldn't be it! That skinny pain in the fanny. Maybe he had been on the game too long, alone too much. Incredible that the thought would ever occur if he *was* in his right mind.

A serene morning unfolded pale gray fingers on the surrounding hillsides, alerting the birds. The sun, never far over the horizon at this time of year, was coming, but it would be chilly for a while. There was fog yet in the valley, and Claude sent clouds of breath ahead of him as he rode down into where Callie had begun her mining career with a shovel and a pan. Appropriate to the hour, he came slowly, half asleep in the saddle himself until some inner self stirred, set nerves to quivering, and woke him. He looked around and sniffed the air, but at first there was nothing to confirm an alarm.

When he reached the river, he detected a smoky odor. The use of his spyglass didn't reveal much in this murky atmosphere. Breakfast campfires, maybe. Surprising that the bank was so unpopulated. His last view of it had been of claims so close together that you could always see at least one from another.

Reaching the river itself, he let the horse wade in where the current was gentle, in order to drink and soothe its legs. Lounging forward in the saddle, he became aware of a man's body entangled in some branches as it drifted by in midstream. Claude straightened. Boots, dungarees, plaid wool jacket—surely a miner. How had it come so far downstream without anyone seeing and removing it? Miners were not callused in that way; in fact, they were superstitious and would have waded out immediately.

He checked his weapons before starting out along the bank. The first thing he came across was a destroyed encampment that had probably serviced at least three men. The tents were burned down to shreds and ashes, goods and utensils scattered, and an elaborate sluice had been overturned before it was smashed. He dismounted and examined the scene more carefully, the Colt in one hand now.

The soft ground bore myriad foot and hoof tracks, all scrambled together. Signs of struggle and, eventually, blood on small stones and twigs. A final piece of evidence, the claim stakes were gone. Not just pulled from the ground and cast about, but gone. He found traces of them finally in the remains of a fire.

Chapter Fourteen

It was almost 7:00 a.m. Ned was sleeping way past his usual hour of rising. Not only that, he was supposed to be on guard duty. The night before he had eaten more than was wise from their depleted stock and even drunk a little whisky—success had gifted him with martyrdom. Wrapped in a blanket wet with dew, he half sat, propped against the rocky hillside near the basic cut. The shotgun had fallen over beside him, but luckily the safety was on. Any other day, the sun would soon reach his face and wake him, unaccustomed as he was to being warm.

Suddenly the birds stopped singing. There was no sound. A pair of scuffed, muddy boots came close to Ned, then another, and another. No one said anything, but the breathing of several men was audible. The muzzle of a rifle approached the old man's face, even touching the peak of his cap and moving it slightly, but then was withdrawn. The boots went away, creaking in the eerie morning silence.

Claude finally found someone, in a manner of speaking, in his search along the riverbank. A bullet kicked up sand and pebbles several feet away. With aim that bad, he wasn't too concerned.

A quaking voice called out: "Skidaddle, whoever you be!"

Claude waved absently but otherwise ignored him. He was suddenly aware of something far more alarming up in the hills that lined the river.

★ ★ ★ ★ ★

The suspension of life that seemed to hang over Ned, clinging to some expectancy in the air as with the coming of an earthquake where the absence of everything can be more terrible than the reality of anything, lasted several seconds. At a signal a dozen weapons were fired simultaneously, striking and bouncing the old man along the rock wall until, mercifully, they slacked off, allowing the lifeless corpse to flop over and reclaim the earth with its face.

Jorem had fired two guns in the first volley, but with eight shooters going at it with enthusiasm, he realized he might be too close to the victim and jumped back, causing him to giggle. Fat brother Billy and six Swope cousins were part of the fun. Several more rounds were fired into the old man, when he was long gone dead, just for the hell of it. By then everyone was yipping and hallooing. A considerable cloud of acrid smoke formed around the killers and drifted over the body.

Callie burst out of her tent and plunged blindly up the hill to the scene of the carnage, screaming Ned's name. As usual she had slept in her clothes, but was blurry eyed, disoriented, and weaponless. In her confusion she ran physically right into the gang, still screaming. Bouncing off of Jorem without being aware of him, she spun to see Ned and, when it sank in, howled her devastation.

It took the men a moment to recover from the surprise, even though they had known she was there, somewhere, working the claim. It didn't take them long, however, to holster their guns and set out to enjoy the young female who had fallen into their hands like a gift from a vile god. Jorem had promised himself and them a lot. Eight faces lit with the excitement of a Christmas morning in hell.

Callie tried to get to Ned, but one of them grabbed her

by the hair and flung her to another one, who held her tightly around the waist and swung her from side to side, getting warmed up.

"Hot damn, don't she feel good," he enthused, trying to kiss her neck.

"Share! Share!" Billy cried, and she went from one to the other like a flung doll, sobbing, barely conscious of what was really happening, or what it portended for her. She wanted desperately, to the extent that she could think at all, to believe that she was still asleep and this was a nightmare.

When Jorem caught her, she recognized him and pleaded: "Why? How could you do that? He was so old."

"That's why," Jorem said.

Her acuity returned sufficiently for her to try to break out of the circle and run. They pretended to allow it for a while, only to chase her this way and that for sport. When they tired of it, Jorem caught her and dragged her by her hair to a tree, tying her hands behind it.

Doing the knots in back, he told the others: "Daddy give me a turrible wuppin' 'cause of her and her boy friend. I mean to have my revenge on her."

"I'm your brother, I git her next," Billy said.

Several of the others staked out their position in the daisy chain. Callie was beyond crying now; she looked at them like a small animal in a trap, head jerking from one to the other. They were all young, unkempt, unwashed, hairy, some with bad skin and others bad teeth; it was a Grand Guignol of faces with all of them grinning.

Jorem tried to kiss her, but she twisted away, spat on him, and tried to bite—things she had never imagined herself doing to another human being. He yelled angrily and slapped her hard, momentarily stunning her into insensibility.

One of them, looking worried, admonished: “Uncle John don’t hold with rapin’ females, Jorem. It’s irreligious.”

“Mind your own business, Cousin Tyler. You don’t have to do nothin’. Watch the rest of us havin’ our fun and you can do yourself dirty if you want, you little pissant.” He looked around to see if the rest of the boys were laughing. “ ’Sides, nobody has to know. We’ll kill her when we’re through.” There were some gasps at that but no real opposition; some of the boys had already opened their pants.

Jorem ignored them all in pursuit of his own weapon. “I want you all to see this, so I’m gonna do it to her right where she is. I got the pecker for it, honey. You ain’t seen nothin’ like it. Unless you . . .”—he turned to the others grinning—“you don’t think ol’ Jorem’s gonna pop a cherry now, do you? Whooeeee, wouldn’t that be somethin’!”

Callie was becoming aware. Her face took on a fixed horror, yet she didn’t, wouldn’t, cry any more. She began to pray, or not exactly pray but more like calling up the Old Testament as in—“Bring down the fire to burn them while they dance, Lord Jehovah, and let their remains be eaten by jackals.” Hatred and destruction, not tears, made her feel in some sense free.

She began to curse them with every word she had ever heard men use, like there was a demon inside her, the ghost of a longshoreman or lumberjack, or even—Papa. She assailed their height, weight, mental powers, ancestry, their manhood, and the tools they used to prove it. It started as a flow and ended as the roar of a barroom whore. Callie couldn’t recognize herself in any of it, but it was an antidote to shame, an anesthetic, blessedly clouding her mind.

Surprised, the men nevertheless liked it; to their primitive minds it was a diversion and somehow erotic. They laughed, slapped their thighs, and encouraged her. She went on cursing them anyway, because nothing they did or felt had anything to do with her any more.

Jorem tore loose her shirt, exposing a lot of her considerable breasts, but didn't pause to bother them in his mad rush to get her pants down around her ankles. First he had to struggle with the belt buckle, fingers numbed by lust, and after that the layered underclothes. And all the time trying to rub up against her—after all, hadn't he promised the boys a boner for the ages?—but it felt awkward, off balance, pushing his groin so far forward of the rest of him in order to meet the curve of the tree and Callie's twisting body. It was difficult to look, much less feel, masterful this way.

He slapped her once and screamed for her to—"Hold still!"—but Callie's struggles only increased.

Then came a fatal mistake. One for which Claude, lying prone in some shrubbery on the crest of the hill above them, had been praying as hard as Callie. Whereas, *he* hadn't prayed in ten years. Looking on for the last several minutes, his sense of helplessness had reduced him to chewing on his lip until it bled.

He had climbed up from the valley and ridden across the top of a ridge until the moment when he came to see several men about fifty yards below on the hillside where piles of rock and dirt and items of equipment indicated a digging site. They were involved in some tumultuous activity down there, but the nature of it wasn't clear because Callie, in her unisex work clothes, failed to stand out in the swirl.

He dismounted to get a better look with the spyglass. When he finally sorted it out, he found it difficult to restrain himself, but at the same time recognized it was one of those horrendous situations where almost anything you did would probably end badly, end with you hurting the one you wanted to save. If any of that ugly pack tried to rape her, he could easily imagine himself driven to fire away with everything he had, and billy-be-damned. Maybe even charge down the hill with both pistols. Yet, if he started shooting, she would still be tied to that tree, fully exposed while some of them were behind cover. Any of them could kill her at will, or threaten to kill her if he didn't give up the fight. Then what?

Sweating without even being in the sun, the moisture on his body was attracting flies. His heart was heard outside his chest, something he had never experienced on his most dangerous robberies. However had he gotten into a dilemma like this? He didn't recognize himself; all this improvident virtue was something he had sought to evade his whole life.

"It ain't gonna work standin' up," Jorem complained down below, "even with my famous ding-dong, I cain't do it. Unloose her there, I gotta do it to her on the ground. You can all still see."

Cousin Tyler, who didn't mind a little killing but had worried about the rightness of rape, was first to comply. He cut the rope behind the tree, throwing Callie forward into Jorem's arms. This simple choice of a sexual position, of comfort and control, changed everyone's lives.

Claude suddenly believed in God, like Callie in the one who destroyed whole cities at a yawn. No doubts now about what to do. Under his breath he even murmured a fervent: "Hallelujah." But then he saw Tyler come around the tree with the hunting knife still in his hand and had no way of knowing what was intended.

The first round ripped into the kid's belly and conferred an automatic sentence of death by geography. Tyler staggered a bit but didn't go over. Looking down at himself, perplexed, startled, as if he had inadvertently wet his pants. The stain that appeared and spread rapidly between his navel and his crotch, however, was very dark. He shook his head in denial. After all, the initial sound had been only a *crack* somewhere up on the hill, indistinguishable from the breaking-off of a branch by the high country winds. It couldn't be what it looked like.

No one else reacted either, it requiring, as it did, a whole different sensibility than that involved in lust. Jorem did let go of Callie, but even she simply stood there. Several heard Tyler grunting and studied him, trying to get a grip on why. When a scream formed in the dying man's throat and began its rise, along with another round coming in at Jorem but whistling behind his head, everyone panicked and either scrambled for cover or dove for the ground where they were.

Everyone but Callie who remained upright, looking around in confusion.

"Callie, damn you! Up here! It's me. Run!" This was followed by a fusillade from the Remington, not trying to hit anything in particular, just trying to keep everyone preoccupied.

It took Callie another few seconds of looking uphill. She didn't see anything except tiny puffs of gunsmoke, but it seemed to orient her. When she got her pants up and did run, it was as though she had been fired out of something. Always a fast runner, able to beat most of the boys in school, and now more motivated than ever before in her short life, she went straight up a steep rocky hillside covered by thorn bushes with very little grace but at fantastic speed.

A couple of shots were fired wide at her out of frustration, but she wasn't even aware. Scraped, torn, and bleeding, when she arrived at the top, she threw herself on Claude in gratitude.

He was reloading the Remington, and yelled—"Hey! Get off!"—so distracted he failed even to register the blazing fact of Callie Fisk deliberately imposing her body on his.

"Get off," he repeated, shaking her free so he could roll a couple of feet away to a new firing position. As soon as he had a target, he began shooting again, but with more deliberation.

She wanted to kiss his cheek. "Oh, dear Lord! Thank you. Thank you. It was. . . ." He pushed her away again, but she scarcely noticed. "It was so terrible. I thought I was going to die . . . and I was so scared . . . but so mad. . . . Those bastards! Those sons-of-bitches, I hope you kill them all."

That got his attention. He stopped firing long enough to see who was lying next to him. The firing picked up from below. "Keep down, for Christ's sake," he barked at her. "More likely they'll kill us. When they get their heads clear, they'll spread out and start coming up. Get on the horse. I'll hold 'em back." He started another reload. Seeing her hesitate, he shouted to get going.

As soon as she was mounted, he fired two more rounds, and then ran to join her, scrambling on in front. The horse was a little confused by having two riders and needed a kick to get it started. Callie almost fell off and had to hang on tightly to Claude as they lumbered away.

"Can he carry two of us?" she shouted into his ear.

Claude didn't bother to answer, and didn't have one anyway. He was busy jettisoning everything he could reach, including his saddlebags. Instead of going along the top of the ridge, he steered them down the back of it and headed east. The only hope he could foresee lay across the Canadian border.

Jorem had to roust some of his boys out of hiding, but once they saw that they weren't going to be cut down by an unseen enemy like poor cousin Tyler, who lay moaning and spilling out his life's blood in front of them, they regained their enthusiasm.

Yet before they could start, there was the question of their dying relative. Jorem wouldn't hear about any course of action other than one that "got his girl back" and killed the bastard who had killed one of their family. That, he said, was a sacred obligation. They could return for Tyler's corpse later; he would be dead by then and easier to handle.

There was some muttering, but, as he was John Brown's boy, there was no opposing him, until someone remembered—"Gold! There's got to be some gold 'round here, boys, somewheres."

Once the stash was discovered, fought over, and divided, Jorem finally got them started on a cautious climb, leading the horses diagonally up the side of the hill to the ridgeline where it was hoped they would be able to see their quarry.

These problems were a great help to the pursued who managed to get a good lead going while the horse was still fresh. They were well out in the flatland that extended all the way to the border by the time the poor animal began to tire. There was no doubt that they could be spotted from up high. They stood out on the meadow like a spider in a tub. After half an hour of hard riding, Claude stopped to rest the animal. Both climbed off and sat on the grass.

He took out his telescope and surveyed the ground behind. "There they are. Just down off the hill."

"I thought maybe they'd give up."

"Not this bunch."

"What do they want? I can't be that . . . special to them."

"You're a woman."

"Oh, Lord. You have to promise to give me one of your pistols. I intend to kill as many as I can and then shoot myself."

"Don't go getting like this is a story on the stage." He stood and folded the telescope. "I thought like that I'd've been dead a long time ago. Mount up."

She got goose bumps holding onto him, but Claude was scarcely aware of her. The horse was getting all the attention, lots of patting and encouraging words, although if it showed any indication of less than maximum effort, it got the boot, too. Claude liked animals, but he liked himself better and was prepared to ride it into the ground.

Seven of the marauders were coming at a complacent gallop behind them. They had seen that their prey were two astride and knew they would catch up, so were relaxed, enjoying the game, joking obscenely among themselves, chewing, smoking, spitting. One smoked a pipe in the saddle, another wore a stovetop, a third a too big (and too warm now that the sun was out) bear coat, causing him to sweat profusely.

Claude's horse, despite everything he could do, had slowed.

Callie shouted in his ear: "How soon before they catch us?"

"If we can just get to the border over there . . ."—he pointed ahead—"Mac's post's somewhere on the other side."

"What if he isn't there?"

"Some ventures don't end well."

The Swope boys came on, closing the gap. By comparison, their horses seemed perfectly fresh. Even at a gallop, one cousin was trying to get something out from between his teeth with a hunting knife. Occasionally he would miss and bleed down the front of his leather vest.

"I think I smell her perfume," Jorem said, brightening.

"She ain't gonna wear no perfume out here," another said. "You seen how she was dressed like a boy."

"Don't you worry, Cousin Caleb . . . we get them clothes off her quick, you'll know she's a female. Didn't you see them muffins?" He got the expected chortles all around and everyone urged their horses to go a little faster.

"Hell," Billy called ahead to his brother, leading the pack, "that's her pussy willow you smell, Jorem!"

"That hill there," Claude panted, it being a sympathetic effect from urging on the struggling horse with his whole nervous system. "Other side of the creek . . . Canada. I don't know if there's a bridge, but maybe it's fordable. . . ."

Callie looked behind, something she had avoided. "They're awful close."

"I know." He dug into the horse cruelly, and it managed to lurch forward a little faster. When they heard the bunch behind begin to hurrah, close enough to indulge in a little shiveree, Claude knew the chase was over.

"It's no good," he told her, reining in abruptly. The horse had been urged forward for so long and suffered so much, it had trouble stopping and reared, almost dumping Callie who had to cling desperately. Claude was off the instant its hoofs came back to earth, with the Remington in one hand.

"I'll hold 'em here."

"No, Claude. I'll stay with you. . . ."

He handed up his Smith & Wesson, shouting over her: "If you don't find Mac, keep going." She tried to dismount, but he gave the horse a powerful whack on the rump, and it, seemingly thrilled with the lightened load, found new life, almost galloping, Callie again struggling to stay on and gain control.

Claude just had time to jam a couple more rounds into the chamber and assume a firing stance. It was necessary to stand because the spring growth in the meadow was thick and tall, and, if he stayed down in it until they were on top of him, he would likely only get one and the rest would ride right over him. He could see them clearly. They were easily in range if only he were a better shot with a rifle. Several had their pistols out, but he wasn't afraid of that—yet.

What he had most feared, happened. They began to fan out on either side. These outriders would surely pass beyond range and catch Callie either on this side of the creek or just beyond. There was nothing he could do to stop it. If only they could have made it to the border. . . .

Claude swung to his right and fired twice at a figure he thought was Jorem, but the rider kept right on, moving even farther away on the circumference of his effectiveness. Then he realized that he had no choice but to deal with the three coming directly at him. He fired again and missed; now, as they closed, zigzagging a little, they were beginning to shoot back with their pistols. However inaccurate, it was a lot of bullets coming his way. Glancing to each side—one man was coming from each of those directions. That made five bearing down. If they pressed the attack, he might get one, maybe two, but these were crazy young bucks who felt impervious and would likely keep coming on.

He felt sweat running down the back of his neck, and then into his eyes as he tried to sight. After a whole lifetime of avoiding corners, he had put himself in a position where it was stand and die. He dropped the rifle and reached for his Navy Colt—better to go with an old friend in hand.

He heard the distinctive crack of another rifle in the distance. Possibly one of the gang had dismounted and was firing at him to keep him down until the others could get close. But then he looked ahead to see the horse of one of his attackers was staggering like a midnight drunk, the rider falling this way and that until finally he went down with it. The other two pulled up, looking around, sensing that the shot had not come from Claude, and there was some new threat here.

Claude looked around with them, as surprised as his pursuers. It had been an incredible shot if it came from . . . ? There was someone on the hill across the border, someone who had stepped out of the trees and was holding a rifle high in the air with both hands, pumping it up and down.

That was enough for Claude; he began to leg it toward the border. It was a long way, and, if any of the wild men decided to stop and use a rifle, they wouldn't have any trouble picking him off. Determined, they might still ride him down.

But he hadn't run ten yards when he looked up, and here came Callie, probably riding faster than ever she had in a lifetime of plow horses back in Vermont. Riding "like the devil's handmaiden" came into Claude's mind from a Pentecostal upbringing.

The outriders, alarmed by the loss of one of their own, called a halt to their encircling movement. That had given Callie time enough to return and pick up Claude, who swung on behind her.

The gang, seeing Claude remounted, resumed their charge. Even the man, who had had his horse shot out from under him and was limping badly, staggered toward the creek, firing his pistol wildly on the run. Mac fired again and knocked one man's hat off, came close enough to another to turn and head him in the other direction.

By that time, the fugitives were frantically splashing through the creek to the other side. Callie even whacked the horse a couple of times and controlled the reins without regard for comfort. They climbed the bank and went on up the hill. People were still firing at them, and, occasionally, Mac answered from above. Callie adroitly steered them into the trees so they got a moment's respite from being a target.

The horse topped the hill, wheezing and coughing, and died. Claude and Callie went down with it hard and lay in a heap, unwilling as well as unable to move. Callie's legs proved to be wedged under a thousand pounds of noble horseflesh. Mac, with his Lee-Enfield in one hand, came running along the crest to help. Bullets cracked close, chipping rocks around his feet, and Claude yelled for him to get down.

When the Mountie reached them, he was, with his remarkable strength, able to lift the horse long enough for Claude to pull Callie from beneath it. Dragged clear, she went on lying there flat on her back, arms outspread, trying to catch her breath.

"You all right, lass?"

She managed a grim smile. "Just . . . worn . . . out, scared."

Claude stood and looked below. "Jesus Christ, they're right behind us. Two at the creek already. Quit moonin' over her and come on."

Mac put a round in the chamber as he marched over to see. "Watch your language in front of the lady."

"She cusses worse than I do now."

Mac looked down the hill and fired.

"How in hell'd you miss that shot?" Claude asked.

"Maybe you might want to do a bit of it yourself," Mac said, scowling while he squinted along the barrel at another target.

Claude pulled out the Colt and fired, but it was still difficult shooting for a pistol. Both of them had to stand in order to shoot over the cusp of the hill. The gang below was coming together, four abandoning their horses and beginning to move upwards like skirmishers, using trees and rocks for cover to good effect. Three were using rifles.

Jorem broke cover, running, and Mac fired again and missed again. "Damn!"

"There's one out on each flank," Mac warned. "They could get behind us."

"That's all I can do with a pistol. The one, you shot his horse, he's hurt but he's still coming."

Mac shot again. Missed.

"Judas Priest," Claude said, "what's wrong with you?"

"Hold your horses," Mac said irritably, but he continued to grimace. "I can see 'em better now."

Callie came over, a little wobbly but hefting the gun that Claude have given her as if she had every intention of using it.

"Are you fit?" Claude asked her.

"I'm all right. Where are they?"

"What are you going to do with that?" he asked her.

"Shoot them . . . when they get close enough."

"Miss Callie, get down!" Mac said emphatically. "This is no bargain for a lady." He fired again and cursed beneath his breath.

When he reached up and squeezed his eyes hard with two fingers and a thumb, Claude had a revelation: "Your spectacles! For God's sake, man . . . you can't shoot without your spectacles. Get 'em on before we're all stretched out."

Mac looked down at his rifle, then up to glare at Claude. Under his breath out of the corner of his mouth he muttered: "Not in front of her."

Just then a fusillade came in from the boys below while the one who was climbing up on the right flank stopped to fire a round that almost hit Callie, striking the tree beside her head.

She ducked, and both men cried—"Look out!"—after the fact. Claude reached over roughly to push her down and hold her there despite her protests.

Mac, frustrated and furious about what had almost happened, jammed his spectacles on his nose, slammed a round into his rifle, spun, and fired at the man out on the right flank, who had reslung his weapon in order to climb higher. Mac's bullet went through his arm into his chest where it pierced the lung. He stood up tall, arching his back as if he had been hit in the front, and fell over sideways, tumbling down the hill, rolling until the rocks caught him.

Mac whirled around, reloading as he did, and fired at the more circumspect climber farther out on the left, who probably thought he was beyond rifle range. It wasn't as successful as with the other, but it removed two fingers from one hand and caused him to reconsider his whole rôle in the chase. The next time he came into view he was scrambling down the hill twice as fast as he had come up.

This brought Claude and Callie to their feet, cheering. With renewed confidence they stood tall and fired steadily at the men who had been advancing directly toward them.

Callie punctuated her shots with challenges shouted in a firm loud voice: "C'mon, you sons-of-bitches, come on up here! I've got a gun now. Try and do those things to me now!" Unaccustomed to revolvers, hers bucked like a bronc' and sent most of the six rounds buzzing through the tops of trees. It didn't matter; the mere fact of shooting it off seemed to give her a great deal of satisfaction.

Mac was so stunned by her language that he forgot to

fire for a moment, but Claude's flurry of six shots was more effective in that they brought a satisfying cry of pain from below.

Proof that they were suddenly winning the struggle could be seen in the fact that only three desultory shots came back, and then some yelling between the men down there that had a despairing ring to it, and sounds of scrambling and falling. Mac dared to stride over the rim of the hill for a look, and reported back: "They're running."

"Quick, give me some more bullets," Callie said to Claude, her voice thick.

Instead, he moved off to join Mac, who was still looking down. "Waste of ammunition," he told her over his shoulder.

"No, damn you to hell! Give them to me."

"They're across the creek, in American territory."

She came up to meet them, waving the revolver dangerously. "I'm an American. I can shoot anyone I want."

Claude pushed the pistol away, then physically urged her back. "Go sit down. Rest. They're out of pistol shot, anyway."

"They can't be. We'll go after them." But she didn't; she did what Claude suggested and flopped down on the ground, exhausted by the exercise of her own passion. She rubbed her head, as if trying to discover what was in there that had made her act the way she had.

"She's . . . ?" Mac, bewildered, didn't even know how to pose it. "What did they do to her?"

"It's more what they had in mind to do," Claude responded.

On the other side of the creek, the gang, some needing help, had regained their horses. They rode off across the meadow with their heads as low between their shoulders as nature allowed. Back to Dogtown to make their report, some of it true.

Chapter Fifteen

Callie refused to do anything or go anywhere until she returned to the dig and gave Ned a proper Christian burial. This was bound to be a long trek since they had only Mac's horse between them, but nothing could dissuade her. In that case, the men had no choice; the countryside was too dangerous after what had happened for anyone to go it alone.

Claude had jettisoned everything he was carrying during the pursuit, and the only item they could find in that vast meadow was the Remington. Mac's cabin, it turned out, was actually several miles upriver. That left what he customarily packed when on patrol, two blankets (for three people), a canteen, a flask of whisky, some hardtack, and reindeer jerky from last winter, and some candy twists which he normally kept in pocket for children but now shared before they started.

The men wanted Callie to ride, but she resolutely refused, maintaining that she was quite capable of keeping up with them on foot.

When they rested before setting out, the men each took a swallow from the flask. Mac claimed it had a medicinal purpose. Claude said many a man's life had been saved by a "quick snort" when they found themselves caught out in harsh conditions.

Callie said, in that case, she wanted her "quick snort," too. Claude handed it over. She drank, coughed a little, put her hand to her chest, and said: "Oh, my, that's strong. But

I can see where it could be useful in pepping you up."

The men exchanged glances. Both wondering, perhaps, on the Day of Judgment would they be found responsible for this?

Starting after the noon hour meant they wouldn't make it to the site in time to do what had to be done, that is, bury Ned and whoever else they found, even though there would be some light all night at this time of year. They moved slowly, the excitement and menace of the morning having consumed their collective adrenalin ration for days to come.

It was decided to camp on the far limits of the meadow at the onset of the long twilight. Callie finally admitted that this day had left her exhausted. The men dug a deep pit for a fire in order to hide it from view, and kept the fire itself small. It was sufficient for coffee, but there wasn't a lot of heat from it, and the night was going to be chilly.

Dinner was jerky, hardtack, and coffee. Afterwards they sat almost on top of the fire pit, extending their hands and feet in order to get them warm, nipping, all three of them, at the whisky as "dessert." Callie had stopped coughing with every sip, but her face did turn pink.

Since they had only the two blankets, Claude said he would take the first watch and keep moving, so he wouldn't be needing one. Mac handed Callie hers and took the other himself. They stretched out as close to the fire pit as possible, but Claude said, now that it had served its purpose, they should let the fire itself die down; in the increasing dark it was probably viewable by anyone high enough in the hills.

Callie managed to be quiet for a few minutes, then complained about the cold.

"Go to sleep and you won't feel it," Mac suggested patiently.

"I'm too cold to go to sleep. And if I did, the sound of my teeth rattling would wake me."

"It's not that cold!" Claude called over less patiently from where he was sitting on a rock, looking cold himself.

Mac was trying to sleep in spite of them.

"What do sourdoughs do out on the trail in winter if they can't have a fire?"

"Huddle with one of their dogs," Claude said. "Sometimes it's a two-dog night. Little bit o' paradise for the fleas, but it's better than freezing."

"What if they don't have dogs?"

"Well, if there's more than one in the party they huddle together."

"Oh?" There was a potent silence, before Callie asked: "Mac, would you huddle with me . . . I'm freezing."

The Mountie, his mind befuddled by near-sleep and half-dreams of living in a little cabin with Callie rocking and knitting on the other side of the fireplace while he rocked on the other, reading Bobbie Burns, came partway back to utter a muffled: "Cuddle?!"

"Huddle!"

"Oh." He felt his smile was probably ridiculous when he said—"I wouldn't mind."—but it was the best he could manage.

Callie was quick to pick up her blanket and move over to slide under Mac's, leaving a certain amount of space between them, naturally. "This way we've got two blankets."

Mac was still befuddled, although it was no longer by sleep; he thought that now he might truly be dreaming. If this was the changed Callie, maybe it wasn't so bad. On the other hand, he had no idea what was expected of him.

Claude looked upon this by-play with a scorn he didn't feel, it being difficult to scorn that in which you yourself long to share. He came over, ambling to show a pretended indifference. "You two look silly, you know that. It's not any two-dog night tonight."

Mac said smugly: "Feels like it under here."

"No," Callie said, "Claude's right, it's not a two-dog night." Mac was on the brink of being crestfallen, but Callie went on: "It's more of a three-dog night, if you ask my opinion."

Claude appeared to consider this, but fooled no one. "Now that you point that out . . . ," he said rather too quickly, and then had to reconsider. "I'm on guard duty, though."

"You could bring your pistol and keep your eyes open, couldn't you?"

"Whoever heard of a laying-down sentry?" Mac complained.

Callie ignored him, telling Claude: "I hope you don't think I'm too bold, but. . . ."

"No," Claude reassured her, "I don't think that. You want to get between us for our body heat, is that it?" He squatted next to them.

"That's a swell idea."

"Just don't you lay too close, bucko," Mac said.

"Just you take care of your side of the blanket, bucko."

"There's a time to be gentlemen," Callie warned, "and a time to be practical. And nobody gets a kiss good night until I'm warm."

Claude quickly slipped beneath the blankets.

"Now . . . ," Callie started to say.

"You'd kiss two strange men laying under a blanket?" Mac asked in the tone of an aggrieved parson. Could he respect this Callie?

Claude groaned.

"I don't see that we're exactly strangers, Sergeant MacDonald, if you want me to call you that?" Callie said loftily.

He had to admit: "When you put it that way, it doesn't sound so bad."

"You first, then," she told Mac, and rolled over to face him. Then she swiveled her head to find Claude propped up on his elbow, watching, and spoke to him sternly: "You face the other way, Mister Emmett. Your turn'll come." She waited until he complied, before returning to Mac.

He locked his hands behind him, so she did the same. There was also a discreet two feet separating them so each had to crane their necks forward . . . closer . . . closer . . . until finally their lips met. Tenderly but not without feeling. Gradually, delicately, something of the man's strength of body and character transmitted itself through the reticence. Callie was, in fact, surprised by the softness of his lips when he lived such a rough life in such a rough place. Not that she was an expert on lips, but she thought this must be a good thing.

Claude didn't sneak a look, as might have been expected, but he did listen hard. After a while he grew restless and cleared his throat loudly. It had the right effect in reminding Callie what she had promised. Mac's long sigh signaled that his good time had come to an end.

"Now you turn away," she told him, and rolled over to meet Claude. He was a lot closer, in fact, within inches, so that she pulled back a little, although it did make things a little easier. However, when Claude tried to introduce his tongue, she said—"Ugh!"—and hit him in the nose with her fist. But before he could even react, she grabbed his face with both hands and returned to the kissing.

Mac had heard the blow and wanted to know what was happening, but no one answered.

Claude didn't keep his hands behind his back, but rather put one behind her head and the other between her shoulder blades, then slid that one rapidly southward. When his pelvis touched hers that was the end of it. She murmured—"Damn you!"—largely because he was forcing her to end it, and she didn't want to. Just as well, her face was burning and she was beginning to wonder if a girl's hair could ever catch fire doing these things, while Mac was questioning why it was taking so long on that side of the blanket.

All three flopped onto their backs, smiling at the sky, and were silent for a moment.

Finally Callie whispered: "Oh, Mama, your daughter's in danger of havin' fun."

On either side of her there was chuckling.

"Which was best?" Claude asked.

"It was a draw." She watched the stars coming out, her own face still glowing brightly. All the stars conceivable up here, even more than in Bent Creek, flickering on like Christmas candles against the watery blue firmament. The sun merely napping along the horizon.

Callie began to sniff and wrinkle her nose; something had broken in on her reverie.

"When was the last time you gentlemen had those shirts and these blankets to a laundry?" she asked quietly, in case they were asleep.

Neither wanted any more conversation. Mac muttered—"Isn't any . . . laundry."—and began to snore.

Claude said: "Nearest's two, three hundred miles. . . ."

Callie was content to let them settle in after that. She had found something in the early stars, an idea that made her want to get up and dance like Wild-Water Ned. But she didn't; it was for the future, so she folded it to her bosom and took it to sleep with her. There it was safe for a while.

In the morning, they went up and buried Ned. Someone had returned and taken away Cousin Tyler's corpse, unless it had been dragged away by a large predator. Either way, they were grateful. Callie insisted on a cross bearing the old man's name and date of death, at least.

"What's his last name?" Mac asked.

"He couldn't remember."

"What was his age?" Claude asked.

"He didn't know that, either. Just carve 'old.' "

Claude asked if there was "one of those lines" between Wild and Water?"

"A hyphen, yes."

Along with the old shotgun, Callie found the Bible she had picked up in Skagway amongst her scattered belongings. Episcopalian, but there was no way of knowing what Ned's religion might have been, anyway. She announced peremptorily that she was about to do the burial service. The men objected, claiming that they had never heard of such a thing as a woman preacher.

Callie said she had the Bible, she went to church, and Ned was *her* special friend and defied the other two to contradict her. "Take your hats off, for goodness' sake."

They did.

"Bow your heads. Or kneel, if you're going to pray. You two raised in a barn?"

They bowed their heads, and Callie began: " 'I am the resurrection and the life, saith the Lord; he who believeth in me, though he were dead, yet shall he live; and whosoever liveth and believeth in me shall never die. . . .' "

When it came to the point of sprinkling holy water on the grave, she borrowed Mac's flask and used it without a qualm, saying it was probably the only thing they held sacred, the two of them. Anyway, Ned would like it.

Mac whispered to Claude: "You notice, she's learned sarcasm?"

". . . earth to earth, ashes to ashes, dust to dust. . . ."

They had wrapped him in his parka and a blanket and threw all of his personal possessions into the grave, his rabbit's foot, ancient pistol, empty poke, clothes, and, Callie insisted, the mining tools.

When it was over, they walked over to the hillside and stood there in silence for a while, looking out at the vivid green and flowered valley as an antidote to death.

"You file on this claim?" Claude asked.

"Ned was going yesterday morning to do that, but. . . ."

"Doesn't matter then."

Mac said, shaking his head: "I should've gone after them."

"*You* should've?" Claude said.

"It's my job, bucko."

"Not in this country, it isn't. What would you've done if you'd caught up with them? . . . you can't hit anything close."

Callie said, trying to cut it off: "It doesn't matter."

"That's a new one," Claude said, "gold doesn't matter."

"That's because it's all you think of," Mac told him.

"No matter how hard you try, *Clarence,* you're not going to make poverty sound noble."

"Clarence . . . that's low."

"You deserve it with all that sanctimonious stuff."

"You wouldn't think it was sanctimonious if you read the Good Book now and then."

"For the love of Mike, I'm sick of listening to you two. We'd better find some horses. I know mine will be around here somewhere because he's too dumb and too old to do anything but eat."

As predicted, Callie's no-name horse and mule were found where she had left them, untethered, munching grass down at the base of the hill. Neither Claude nor Callie had any use for the mule. Mac said he would take it back to his post and give it to someone down on their luck.

Half an hour later Cousin Tyler's mount ambled in as if looking for company. Claude tried him, and he seemed capable.

Among Ned's rag-tag collection of things, they found a can of pineapple and one of corned beef. Callie acted as if she had known of this little cache all along, but the men weren't fooled. Mac said it was in keeping with the ingrained habits of an old sourdough. Or, if he was that old, maybe he had just forgotten he had it.

At any rate, they had some welcome variety in their lunch, sitting on the grass of a rocky outcropping, Callie scheming and planning, and the other two wondering what it was that caused her to be so contemplative, which was not like her gabby self. Marveling, too, at how quickly she had adapted to whisky as the wine of the North. True, she sipped hers, but without a sign of pain.

Mac broke the mood. "Callie, I've got to go back to my post."

"I know. It's about time."

"You don't think the less of me for it?"

"I admire it. We all have a duty to something or someone. Except Mister Emmett here."

"That's not fair. I got a duty . . . to my ancient profession. And what's your duty, *Miss* Callie, if you're all done prospecting?"

"I don't see as it's any of your business, Mister Emmett. Since you're so obviously not going to be a part of it."

"Callie," Mac blurted, interjecting himself by moving

around partially to mask Claude's presence, "I wish he wasn't around to hear me say this, but it seems he's always around when we're together." He took an almost debilitating swallow of air before he leaped in. "I'd leave the force for you. We could live in Dawson or even Winnipeg, if you wanted. Buy a saloon. I'd be a real solid man for you, Callie." He exhaled gratefully.

She shook her head, avoiding any view of Claude, who wisely contained himself. "I wouldn't let you do that, Mac, throw away your career, your whole life."

"I want to. I . . . I . . . *like* you," he blurted. "You're a wonderful girl."

Claude did groan at this, but softly. Callie leaned around to give him a look that should have left a bruise on his conscience. He got the message, stood, showed his back with hands clasped behind, and pretended to be absorbed by the scenery.

"Even so," she told Mac gently, "I can't. You're a very nice man, but I have responsibilities, too. Lots of them, to the people back home, to Ned, to myself, and I'm going to fulfill them."

"What do you mean? Where?"

"Back in Dogtown."

Both men gawked. Claude felt free to come over. "You can't go back there," Mac entreated. "They'll do something terrible to you. Come with me, you'll be safe in Canada."

"Then I'll be safe in Dogtown . . . that's in Canada."

For a moment Mac didn't know how to respond.

Claude did. "She's stuck on that again."

"Mac, it's true. I talked to some U.S. Army surveyors who're doing whole new maps of the territory. They told me the real border's that dry creek on the other side of town. That means we could be in Canada right now. All the gold around here belongs to Canada. The Putney Library was right."

"What's that got to do with my l-liking you."

"If you told your commander, it could mean the end of the Swopes. There's no law to stand up to them the way things are."

"If I was to tell my commandant this, I wouldn't have to worry about resigning. I'd bloody well leave on the toe of his boot." The mere thought of it was raising a gorge. "They'd say I was daft. You'd make me the laughingstock of the fort. Is that what you want? Maybe you're laughing at me now." Despite Callie's heartfelt denials he got up and stomped back to the campsite.

Callie, because she was beginning to know something of men, guessed that his temper had little to do with geography and everything to do with wounded male pride. Men forced these things on you. They were such odd creatures when you understood them, always claiming to be more logical, reasonable, balanced. What hooey!

"All right," Claude said, turning and coming back to stand over her, "what *are* you going to do?"

"Become a business woman."

"A business *woman!*"

"It's a frontier, isn't it? People can be anything they have the courage to be."

In an alarmingly intimate manner, Claude sat close to her, inclining his head toward her ear and lowering his voice. "Honey, I got enough right now to open my own bank. I don't have to be out on the trails. We could go somewhere warm. Be business men together. You could keep the books or something. Anyway, we'd be respectable and very, very comfortable."

"Is this another proposal of marriage?"

"Well . . . yes. . . ." His voice grew fainter. "Yes, dammit."

"Don't believe him, lass," Mac called, coming over. "The man never kept a promise in his life."

Under his breath, Claude said: "Jesus, he can hear a rabbit in the snow at a hundred yards. Can you imagine what it would be like to live with a man who can do that?"

Callie, the eternal referee, bolted to her feet. "You two!" she fumed. "You're so used to buying females you don't have the faintest idea how to court one. I'm not a horse up for auction. Neither one's ever said you loved me." She waved her finger at them. "Don't deny it, I keep count and the score's zero to zero. That by itself makes you a mighty pitiful pair of suitors, so, I'll just make my way on my own, thank you."

"I know," Claude said, all the fight gone out of him, "and you got a will of iron."

" 'Bout time you noticed."

Chapter Sixteen

The realization that he was rich had continued to prey on the mind of the Blue Parka Man. He found himself wondering how the rich spent all day every day if they weren't, say, planning hold-ups. That was probably it; they went back to work in order to earn more money . . . and more . . . and. . . .

The thought depressed him. If he followed that example, he would surely hang. Or worse, if a drunken mob got a hold of him. And if he was honest with himself, he would have to admit that the thrill was wearing off. He needed an objective, a purpose to his life. Any fool could have one of those—why couldn't he? Maybe Callie could tell him; she had answers for everything else. On the other hand, did he want to hear it?

Mac, too, was despondent at the time of leaving, dreading the isolation that awaited him at the cabin. He made no further attempts to sway Callie, but she felt badly and gave him an embrace that included a sweet kiss which cheered him a little. The men shook hands and punched each other's shoulders.

Mac wished them both luck in such a way as to imply a doubt on his part that they would meet again, then rode slowly down the hill to cross the flatlands. Back to his duty to Queen and Country, and. . . .

Claude just happened to mention that he was headed in more or less the general direction of Dogtown himself, so asked if he might not ride along with Callie for a spell. She had no objection, as it was hard going for her old horse that was always at risk of breaking down. He hadn't told her yet, but Claude had decided to see it through with her. Whatever she was up to. Ride right into Dogtown, bold as winter, even if it was madness. Right now he needed a little madness.

But he could hardly do it on Cousin Tyler's horse, so they sought out a cabin just below the treeline that provided sanctuary to anyone who found themselves catty-corner to the law. There they sold it for practically nothing, warning the new owner not to ride it anywhere near Dogtown, threw Callie's nag into the deal, and bought two new ones.

They rode side by side, talking all the while, on a sunny, windy day with Dogtown up ahead across relatively easy terrain, reachable by early afternoon. Claude reasoned that it would be good to get there before too many got drunk.

"Just what the hell is a French laundry, anyhow?"

"That's to let people know it's not an American laundry."

"How's it different?"

"It's French."

"I see. It's more continental, fancier because it comes from Europe."

"That's right."

"And you expect me to put up money for this?"

"Somebody's going to."

"What kind of equipment you expect to find up here?"

"At first, the good old-fashioned kind, washboards, ringers, and steam irons. Whatever I can find or put together. Nothing wrong with them. I've done a lot of washing and ironing with them myself."

"Where you going to get starch?"

"One food there's no shortage of in the Yukon, potatoes."

"What if people want to stay dirty?"

"I'm not concerned."

"No, what you are, Miss Fisk, is cocky. And if you'll forgive me, you're gonna get your little tail shot off."

"If I do, Mister Emmett, your big one'll go right along with it."

Claude burst out in delighted laugher. "I'm having trouble getting used to this you. I mean, you honest to God expect to make money from this?"

"You'll see. But that's not why I'm here. I'm going to have my revenge on these people."

The first thing that greeted them on the main trail into town was a big sign that read: **THE NAME IS DAUGHTON**.

"I think it's a hint," Claude said as they rode past.

Most of the tents were gone, burned out; only a few remained and were occupied. But where were the bold miners who used to come out to look over every newcomer, often greet them, sometimes in humorous or obscene ways but welcoming? Now a few furtive eyes shown.

The whorehouses were still there—backbone of the economy—but the Hole in the Bed had been renamed The Daughton Revelation. Swopes, none of whom had taken up mining and obviously but easily identifiable by their resemblance to gargoyles, seemed to be everywhere, strolling armed, sitting on the porches of the whorehouses with rifles or shotguns across their laps, standing around the livery stable, staring at the couple riding in.

"Like a prison with all guards and no prisoners," Claude noted. "A lot quieter, I'll say that."

"Perfect," Callie said.

"What are you so happy about? The fact that the fun is gone . . . yeah, you'd like that."

The few women, miners, and tradesmen on the streets were timid, moving from shelter to shelter, seldom stopping or speaking to one another. The many nationalities and races had disappeared entirely.

As they reached the center of town, Callie suddenly reined in her horse to the point where it bucked and snorted angrily. "Oh, dear Lord."

Claude followed the line from her horrified eyes to the cause: a man hanging from a beam cantilevered out above the entrance to the Northern Lights. His face was black; an enormous swollen tongue protruded. His executioners had placed his feathered hat on his head. Missing were his yellow boots. Crows awaited their chance on the roof.

Spontaneously and for the first time in her life, Callie crossed herself, even though back home it would have been roundly condemned as Papist. She had to look away. "God help me for a poor weak woman."

Claude said: "Me, too. That's a sight always makes me depressed."

"Did you know him?"

"I stood him a drink once. What now?"

Callie didn't have to answer; she merely nodded at someone approaching down the middle of the street. Claude looked to find Jorem, wearing yellow boots, and his brother Billy. Behind them, moving with slightly more *gravitas,* were the two older brothers.

"I cain't believe my eyes," Jorem said, scowling as he put his hand on his pistol. "After what you two done to us?"

Billy, as always a step or two behind and partially shielded by his more lethal brother, said: "This here's our town now, so's we can kill anybody we want to."

Claude moved his hand close to the Colt in his belt while he studied Billy. "I guess you're the moron they got in every big family." He had decided that he might die right here, and it wouldn't be so bad, at that, so long as he could be assured of taking these boys with him and then jumping them again in hell.

"We want to see your father, Mister J. B. Swope," Callie said mildly.

"All the two of you's gonna see," Jorem replied, "is dirt in your face. You ain't ridin' outta here no ways."

The two older brothers, Tom and McNab, came up behind them. "What do they want, Jorem?" Tom asked.

"These two killed Cousin Tyler and Marcus and wounded t'others. They bushwhacked us. Before that they beat me up and had fun o' me. Had fun o' the whole family in front o' the town. Now they got the almighty gall to come ridin' in here like the king and queen o' somewheres. I'm gonna hang 'em."

"Little brother," Tom told him, "that wasn't what you was asked."

"Ain't what I told you enough?" Jorem shouted, so frustrated he kicked dust.

"I came to talk to your father about a business proposition," Callie said. "Bygones could be bygones if you'd let them."

"Not likely," McNab said. "And what's he got to do with it, anyways?"

"I want you to know, Mister Emmett, here, was just escorting me." She turned to Claude. "Thank you ever so much, Mister Emmett. You're free to go on your way now."

That brought a chorus of refusals from the boys, but Claude clearly had no intention of leaving anyway.

He did manage a smile. "Day late and a dollar short, lady."

Callie could only shake her head and murmur: "I'm sorry."

McNab pulled on his ear. "Lemme think on this. You waltzed right in here 'cause you *want* to talk to Daddy?"

Jorem glared at his older brother. "Damn you, McNab, what're you nosin' in for? You ain't king o' ever'body 'round here."

Callie saw her opportunity and jumped. "He's afraid I'll tell your father what he did to me."

Jorem, shouting at her to shut up and stop telling lies, tried to pull his pearl-handled pistol out of its Western holster until the powerful McNab grabbed that arm at the wrist and twisted it, snarling: "What *did* you do, little brother?"

"Nothin'! I didn't do nothin'! You gonna believe her 'g'inst your own kin?"

"Somethin' 'g'inst Daddy's rules?" McNab persisted.

"They killed your blood and tried to git the rest o' us from ambush, her an' him, don't that mean nothin' to you?"

"Mister Mc . . . Mister Swope, we're business men . . . yes, me, too . . . and we've got propositions Dog . . . Daughton needs, if it's to progress into the fine new big city your father obviously intends it to be. Ideas that will enhance the business and civic climate and instill pride in its citizens. So everybody all over the world will hear about it and know this wretched little mining town, this hole in the ground, dirty and crime-ridden, for what it really is, the metropolis of the future, the capital of a nation of gold practically, Valhalla of the great Northwest."

Claude, unbelieving, shook his head and muttered: "That's mighty thick."

McNab looked to his younger brothers. "I don't have a notion in hell what she's talkin' 'bout. Tom, go see what the old man wants us to do to these no-accounts."

Chapter Seventeen

Tom emerged from the saloon/courthouse and signaled for them to come in. Callie and Claude dismounted and, the first crunch point, were ordered to hand over their guns. Claude hesitated, even though he ought to have expected it. Callie implored him with her eyes, and finally he acceded. They had come too far.

As they went, Callie had an opportunity to speak out of the corner of her mouth to Jorem: "You make any more trouble and I'll strip myself naked to show the bruises you put on my private places."

That idea seemed to freeze Jorem with terror. A squeaking—"I won't."—was all he could get out.

They had to dodge around the dangling corpse that was attracting a lot of black flies and becoming odorous, and bear the cawing of the greedy crows. Callie held her breath and kept her eyes on the ground.

"Gettin' ripe," Claude commented unnecessarily.

Inside, the saloon still somewhat resembled the establishment once owned by Slocum. Several desks or clerks' counters had been set up in the open space where formerly card tables rested, and the bar served only wine, the favored drink of the Messiah, Tom informed them. Most of the desks and counters were empty, but two clerks were working diligently.

The old man was sitting at the largest desk, a roll top, in the back of the room, wearing a dealer's green visor that went some little way toward mitigating his Old Testament persona despite the fact that he was dressed all in black. He stood, using his height and removing the visor when he saw them marching toward him.

As they approached, he asked Tom: “You take away their weapons?”

“Yes, sir.”

“Look for boot knives?”

“Yes, sir.” He hadn’t, but hopefully they weren’t carrying any. Around Daddy, denial was usually the safest alternative. If Tom was mistaken and they killed his father, then there wouldn’t be anything to worry about.

“The rest of you, begone.”

Jorem gave Callie a defiant look before, on impulse, pleading: “Daddy, lemme tell you . . . these here’s liars, thieves, and blacklegs, the two of ’em, you can’t believe any. . . .”

“Begone, I said!” It was a roar. Jorem, who felt the wind of his father’s breath on his face, winced and slunk away after the others, competing to see who could get out first.

“Sit.” John Brown Swope indicated two desk chairs nearby; Claude brought them over. The patriarch remained standing, with his feet planted apart and arms crossed in front of him. A string tie peeked through the flowing beard that fell to his arms. Claude noted that he had taken to combing it. Tangled fountains of waves and curls stood out and around his head like a gray sunburst.

“Well, speak.” Every word he uttered sounded like bowls in the Hall of the Mountain King.

Claude started to answer, but Callie interrupted him by standing and crossing her arms in imitation of the old man, her idea of showing that they weren’t afraid. “Would you agree, Mister Swope . . . ?”

“Judge Swope!”

"I'm sorry. Your Honor would agree that cleanliness is close to godliness?"

"Don't you go puttin' words in my mouth, Jezebel. And, anyway, I'm no Quaker or Puritan soft-belly."

"We believe it," Claude spoke up quickly, seeing Callie momentarily set back. He got away with it; the old man took it for obeisance.

Callie tried again, plunging ahead according to her misconceptions. "Didn't our Lord wash the feet of his disciples?"

"I don't wash anybody's feet, young woman. I don't like feet. Who are you . . . standing there in imitation of me, I don't like that, neither . . . some kind of evangelist?"

Callie dropped the arms immediately. "I'm sorry." It wasn't going well.

"Prohibitionist maybe," he went on, "like that Susie Bluenose down in Skagway? She come up here and tries to interfere with business, I'll hang her. Far as I'm concerned business is next to godliness."

"I'm a business man myself, Your Honor. Women can be one, these days, if they've got a good idea, something people want, and it pays a handsome profit, not only for them but for their backers and the whole community, in fact." She had to stop to take a deep breath.

"That so?" was all the old man said.

Claude thought to help and plunked two pokes full of gold on the desk—where they got barely a glance. But when he added that he was prepared to open a bank, back Callie's enterprise, and put up all the cash himself while sharing out the profits, hot coals of greed instantly formed in the patriarch's eyes.

He suggested, more gently this time, that Callie should go on with her pitch. He even sat down so he could figure and doodle on a piece of lined accounting paper.

Callie, trying to stay ahead of his moods, babbled ideas, promises, flattery, and lies, but making it a point never to mention money without tying it, however remotely, to some Biblical reference. Toward the end she was desperate enough to make up quotes and seemingly getting away with it.

Finally her breath just died, leaving her with a half-open mouth and the room in silence. It didn't seem to bother the old man. Claude was happy still to be alive. The old man stared out the window.

"A laundry. Could be. Town wouldn't stink as bad. Might even get a few tourists up here . . . people want to see the gold fields. We could charge an admission to 'em. Let 'em dig or pan for a few minutes. Nobody else is. Tourists'd like to be clean, that's so. We'd have 'em around for the saloons and . . . other amusements. One thing they could count on would be law and order."

Claude was having trouble controlling himself; the idea of Dogtown as a tourist Mecca struck him as hilarious and threatened to pitch him into the pit of no return. A quick dangerous look from Callie, who knew him so well now, discouraged this impulse to self-destruction.

"I don't like banks or bankers," John Brown announced suddenly, turning his scheming gaze full on Claude. "And when it comes down to it, you don't look much like one to me."

"I'd say that's to my credit, wouldn't you? As far as not liking banks, maybe that's because you never had one of your own. Man owns a bank owns a town, and it's real respectable. I'd be willing to go sixty-forty on ownership."

"Who gets the sixty?"

"Well, me," Claude responded. "I supply all the capital.

You need a lot of that to start a bank, and it'd best be in gold, which mine is."

"It's my town already, Mister Emmett . . . we split even."

Claude looked at Callie in simulated despair, since it was no more than what he had expected.

"Why do you want a bank here?"

Claude was ready. "You see, this little lady and me, we met out in the fields. I was looking around for business opportunities, and she was trying to be a miner. I just fell head over heels in love the minute I saw her. . . ."

Callie's mouth dropped open again, and this time her whole face followed. What on earth was the man saying?

Claude went on lying expansively and, Callie thought, all too well. Lying about who he was, his background, and where he had obtained the financing. Refusing to be intimidated by the old man's glare, he batted back every question put to him.

When he wound up, Swope just stared at him. Claude stared back. Callie couldn't help herself; she looked nervously from one to the other to see who would blink first. She had it in her mind that, if it was Claude, they would both die.

Finally John Brown slammed his big fist down on his desk. Callie jumped and gasped. *Oh, my Lord,* she thought, a hand clutching her heart, *he is Papa. He must have died and been reincarnated up here like a Hindu.* Her color drained into the floor as if someone had pulled a plug in her foot. The old man's eyes flashed and flickered like heat lightning in the summer, except that it was a lot more frightening than the real thing.

"You got a serpent's tongue, young man! 'Thou shalt not lie,' saith the Lord God Jehovah. 'Thou shalt not give false witness.' You know what happens to forked tongues . . . they're rooted out. And I doubt that's the only Commandment you've broke. Sittin' here fillin' my ears with false stories, untruths, and golden promises . . . takin' me for a fool." He sat back for a moment and regarded Claude cagily. "You got a boot knife on you?"

"Yep."

Swope didn't look worried. "I knew. What I still don't know is who you are, where you come from, or where you got your money. But you talk smart and got an imposin' way about you, both of you. I'm gonna let you try your ideas. Just remember, there's a whole lot of us and only two of you. You try to flim-flam us and you hang outside here . . . I hang women, too . . . right next to that afterbirth o' Satan on a she-ass, Red Rhuel, who tried to cheat me. Take a good look on the way out. For now, I'll give you the two empty buildings at the end of the next block down other side of the street. Go look at 'em."

Callie got her breathing going again. Claude rose slowly and stuck out his hand. The old man didn't even look at it, turning back to his desk. Claude shrugged, picked up the bags of gold, put his arm around Callie, and urged her out, moving carefully.

"You kill my brother's boy, Tyler, and the other, Marcus?" came the old man's voice out of the back of his head.

"Never heard of them."

"Weren't worth much."

They managed to exit without taking a good look at that "afterbirth o' Satan on a she-ass," and without being the worse for it.

"Claude," Callie whispered on the way out, "I feel like the greatest trickster in the world . . . and I'm not a bit sorry."

"Greatest lure there is . . . respectability. Been more souls sold for that than Helen of Troy."

Callie took up residence in the only boarding house devoid of vice, run by a Quaker lady. Fortunately for her, Swope hegemony had driven away a couple of boarders. Claude, once he found that he was definitely not to share her room, decided to sleep in the new bank building and take his meals at the saloons. For one thing he had bought a large safe in Liarsville and filled it with part of his ill-gotten hoard.

Ever cautious, he had brought it into town by mule in the wee hours of the morning when even the Swope youth with their protean dissipations had exhausted themselves. He unloaded it mostly by himself, although the town half-wit, Jimmy, was employed at this, too.

Setting up *real* businesses turned out to be complicated and full of unforeseen glitches. Paper was a principle shortage; it turned out that most people in mining camps and towns had little use for it beyond answering the call to nature, and in the summer, when plant life was active, they didn't need it even for that.

Staffing was another problem. Fortunately the conduct of the Swope young men, brutal and unwilling to pay, had a depressing effect on the sex industry.

Callie hired a couple of the girls, laid down the law on deportment—no drugs or alcohol on the job, regular hours, no cussing, and dress modestly. She had to pull a few feathers.

Fortunately the miners were used to the girls' high-handed ways. The women themselves seemed to adapt to the regular hours, steady work, and pay. One voiced the idea that it was nice to go into a saloon and get drunk as a customer.

Callie found a few buckets of unopened paint brought in the previous year to tart up a whorehouse and never used. She was taken aback for a moment in that the town was almost entirely gray and the paint was yellow and blue. Then it struck her that this was a gift from God. Soon Jimmy was creating the first varicolored buildings in town and maybe in all of Alaska, a yellow French laundry and a blue bank with white trim.

Claude had trouble accepting the fact of a bank, his bank, being that color; it wasn't dignified, and he didn't know if he would even hold up one that unconventional, but she had the job half done by the time he got out of the saloon one evening, and he was too befuddled to argue.

After that she demanded that he limit himself to two drinks a day, and he, contemplating his blue bank, accepted meekly.

Mac had looked forward to a return to his cabin, to what passed for a home life, hoping it would raise his spirits. A few books, a fire, mail—if he could think of anyone to write to—his housekeeper's cooking and complaining.

Usually people stuck messages in the door cracks or weighted them with rocks on the threshold if they needed Mac for something, but this time there was nothing except a note from a passing trapper who had borrowed some cornmeal (the door was always left open) for biscuits. Inside, the cabin was just as empty. No message anywhere from the housekeeper. He never saw her again.

Without people or dogs he would have to cultivate a squirrel or a chipmunk. He had known men who invited in and treasured rats and mice as someone to speak to during a long winter's isolation. Until they were forced to eat them.

The next night it took almost an entire bottle of Scotch to get to sleep. Mac was not a famous drinker—had not been truly drunk since he was a youth, not suitable for an officer of the Crown—but he kept a ration over the winter to fend off the demons, a wee dram now and then of wonderful nectar from the Isle of Skye, especially to lighten a long Saturday night, always before the beginning of the Sabbath at twelve, of course. As in most years, he had hardly dented what was allowed for troopers in his situation by Dawson.

For the first time in his life he became devotedly, supremely drunk for five days in a row, eating almost nothing. Finally there were no bottles left, no more drams wee or otherwise. All he could remember of it afterwards was singing a hundred choruses of "The Gallant Forty-Twa."

The prospect of returning to sobriety was not entirely a pleasant one. Without the bottle he was alone again.

In the aftermath, Mac went outside, stripped to the waist with his galluses dangling, and put his head in a bucket of very cold water from the well in front. Just then Skookum came out of the woods. He stood waiting patiently in his silent way. What was customarily a dour face had turned observably grave.

When Mac came up from the bucket, sputtering and burbling and shaking his head, he spotted the Indian and jumped. This was unheard of in Mac, who could usually accept any sudden appearance or occurrence, any sudden anything, with perfect equanimity.

The inclination to abstinence had come too late; he saw that in Skookum's face.

"Sergeant, you come soon."

"What is it?"

"Somebody rob, kill Swede." He was referring to a

trapper and hermit who lived seven miles away. "Cut him bad. Blood every part cabin."

Mac was devastated but tried to maintain the discipline Skookum expected of him. He knew the Indian would never reprove him because he would understand its redundancy.

"When?"

"Yesterday."

"You know who?"

"Young whites from there." He pointed in the general direction of Daughton.

Chapter Eighteen

Stealing came as natural to a Swope as to a Gypsy. Now they had stolen an entire town. However, business and administrative skills were not among their strengths. What good was it ultimately to kill a miner and steal his claim if there was no one to work it? Certainly no Swope would, any more than they would stand behind the counter of a store. Obviously they hadn't thought it through.

Travelers had begun to avoid the area, and even new gold seekers went away around if they got the word. The barbarians had conquered, but the Romans were needed to make things run.

Actually the only business in town that was really succeeding was Callie's French Laundry. Banking required trust, and there was little enough of that in Dogtown. Still, Claude got on. He was bored, but he got on, spending most of his free time gambling, hunting, or helping Callie next door. Once he threatened to go back on the game, but she reasoned him out of it by saying that, if he did, she would kill him.

Callie had turned out to have considerable entrepreneurial talent, particularly at advertising. Her time in Alaska had taught her, among other things, that men left to their own devices were perpetual slobs. They dressed up for only one reason, to have a place at the honey pot. Now that the whores were fewer, it meant more competition among the men.

She had hand-printed signs, placards, and leaflets

handed out as far away as Forty-Mile Camp and Lousetown. A novice prospector newly come from Skagway said he had seen one there. **WASH AND WIN A WOMAN** was simple, direct, and perhaps a little misleading, but it served. **LOOK BETTER, SMELL BETTER, DO BETTER, GO TO BED CLEAN, WAKE UP HAPPY** was the sauciest. **CLEANLINESS IS NEXT TO GODLINESS** was thrown in just in case God, or anyone who feared Him, might drop by Dogtown. It was never known to attract a customer.

Showers were added so the prospectors and miners could be "clean from the inside out." Precious perfumes were bargained away from the doves so the men could douse themselves with somewhat diluted versions of it, an enormously popular practice although it occasionally led to accusations of disloyalty and even combat on the part of sweethearts.

Callie worked the front counter herself because that's where the genius lay.

"Hi, there, little lady. Got somethin' here'll give you a trial. Ain't had 'em off in six months, some of 'em."

The old miner laughed long at his own circumstance or shame. Callie never let them feel that it might be shame. He dumped the load of clothes on the counter, and she held them up for inspection.

"Well, Mister Dixon . . . that's your name, isn't it? Blondie Dixon?"

The old man cackled appreciatively and a little hysterically in the manner of people who haven't had anyone to talk to for months at a time, a behavior she had found unnerving when she first came but was quite at ease with now.

"That's right, that's right. I swear I don't know how you know'd that, though I heer'd you know'd ever'body. Hellfire . . . excuse my French . . . I ain't been a blondie in forty years." He grabbed at his tangled mass of white hair and pulled so hard he actually pulled some out, which only made him cackle some more. He held up the hairs. "I'm only fifty years old, would you believe it? Started down in Creede, lookin' for silver. Been all over, been up here since long 'fore there was a rush. Been workin' that glory hole out by Frenchman's Point of late."

Miners came in two types, silent and spouting. Success usually led to the latter. "Ain't slept in three months neither, but I'm rich, by golly. Oh, sweet Annie McFanny I'm rich!" he declared, head back. "Pardon my French again . . . I mean no harm, ma'am."

"I know." Callie, who always wore a dress and apron behind the counter, inspected the pile of filthy clothes with the same smile one might employ admiring the Gobelin Tapestries. "I do believe these dungarees could stand up by themselves." She actually proved her point by standing the pants on their knees which brought whoops of laughter from the customer, Dixon doing a little dance step and pointing accusingly at his own pants.

They never felt embarrassed if you laughed with them. Not only miners, but men in general.

She alarmed him momentarily when she pulled a baseball bat from under the counter and brandished it. "However, I believe we can get them to lay down with this . . ."—she gave the pants a whack and reduced them to a puddle of denim—"and then give them a good scrubbing."

After a moment old Blondie realized it was a performance, recovered, and started laughing again.

Callie pulled the pile together. "Did you go through the pockets?"

"What fer?"

"We find a lot of dust and nuggets in them."

"That sure speaks well o' you, young lady, but don't you worry, there's lot's more where that come from. I got my poke right here, and it's a damn' good 'un." He waved it on high, looking up reverently as at the Assumption. "You don't get it, the bad girls will. Oh, I hope they're bad! I been out there soooo long, and I'm so pent up fer an old feller. You're just welcome to anything you find, lil' darlin', and I hope I wasn't too fresh with you, 'cause I am a devil sometimes when. . . ."

She reassured him and got him started out the door, which was not difficult sincc hc was ncar frantic to begin his debauch. Callie watched him go off down the street, talking to himself still. It made her a little sad; no wonder so many came back with nothing after years of toil and delusion. Diamond Jim Brady for a week, or the time it took them to get to town, then back on the trail with a pick and a pan.

Just the same, she could go through the pockets and cuffs with a clear conscience. The first discovery was a nugget the size of her thumb, and before she was through there were several nuggets and a pile of dust on the counter.

Vera had come out of the back with the scale and bag to look over her shoulder. "You found the best damn' way of minin' gold I ever seen. They gonna make you queen of that Vermont place."

Callie had been sending money home regularly, but now she smiled to herself, thinking of how little she cared about Bent Creek and the ghost of who she had been in that "Vermont place."

Mac had not been back to his base, Fort McKenzie, since spring when he had returned the dogs and picked up his horse. It looked different to him, but then everything did lately. For one thing there were a lot more troopers, a large patrol just having come over from Dawson on an extended exercise.

"I'm determined, sir," he told the commandant, Thursby, "I'm resigning."

"I'm not accepting it, now or in the foreseeable future."

"I have a right to resign the service, sir."

"Hells bells! If this was civilization, yes, Sergeant, you have. But I'm God here."

Every time he was away from the fort for a few months, Mac forgot why they called him Hammer and Tongs, Old Piss and Vinegar, or Bloody Bridles Thursby. It was coming back to him.

"No, by George," the colonel boomed, "I won't have it! You're a bully trooper, son of a bully trooper. Why else would I put you out on that god-forsaken border? Who else could I trust?"

The colonel, his squat body bundled stolidly behind his colonel's desk, looking up at tall Mac standing in front of him at parade rest, felt his normally choleric face reddening to a desert sunrise and his brigadier's mustache begin to quiver at the far ends; these were bad signs. He struggled for control and lower blood pressure.

"I know there's always been those damned silly rumors. You shooting people on sight, if they tried to cross the border, but you'd have to be a lunatic to do that. Anyway, we give it no credence, so I don't want that influencing your decision, you understand me?"

"I left my post to go over to Daughton for almost four days, sir."

The colonel looked down at some papers on his desk, delivering the view that this was all very unimportant.

"You're entitled to five days' leave. Last year you didn't take any."

"I didn't have anywhere to go."

"Didn't take any year before, either. Or . . . have you ever had leave, Sergeant?"

Mac cleared his throat and tried again. "You have my report in front of you. I was drunk for five days and caused the death by violence of a trapper known to me and others only as the Swede. Most likely by the criminal gang over in Daughton, the Swopes. That's a clear dereliction of my duty, sir."

"It certainly is. You're hereby fined fifty dollars to be withheld from your pay at the rate of five dollars a month for ten months. Of course, you hardly ever collect it, anyway. You can stand at ease now, Sergeant," he said looking up abruptly, as if just now noticing Mac's presence.

Mac barely loosened. "For a man's life, sir?"

"You can't know that. You could hardly expect to be everywhere on a hundred-mile stretch of border at the same time. I don't care how sober or drunk you were. Incidentally, don't file a chit for a liquor supply this year, it'll be denied. What you need is a wife. Too long alone over there . . . do it to anyone."

"I'll collect my kit, sir."

"Wait a minute. You still think you're resigning?"

"Yes, sir. Either that or you'll have to lock me up."

The colonel stood and slipped into his avuncular role. Mac still towered over him. "What is it, son . . . a woman?"

"The loss of one."

The colonel took this in and nodded sagely, clasping his hands behind his back and leaning slightly forward like a Hapsburg emperor. "Now I understand . . . I was young. Someone you met over in that so-called Dogtown? No doubt a beautiful girl, eh? I can understand that."

"No, sir. More like passably pretty. When she tries."

That set the colonel back a little. "Well . . . she probably knows a few of those, eh, tricks that some of those women know. Am I right?"

"No, sir. Not the kind you mean. She's very . . . a very good young woman. Pure."

"Pure?" The colonel was becoming desperate for some kind of explanation that suited his preconceptions. "I see, one of those soft, clingy types, all tender on the outside, but. . . ."

"Not exactly. It's more like all hell's loose when she's around. I mean, she's got a lot of agitation in her and, well, opinions, and there always seems to be something happening. For better or worse. Usually worse."

"Damnation, what's wrong with you, Sergeant? I don't . . . can't believe a word you're saying. If you're playing with me. . . ."

"No, sir."

"I'll tell you this, if your father was alive, he'd give you the same advice I'm about to give you. No woman's worth an honorable career. And you'll never find a decent one hanging around over across the border, either. That shiftless, lazy, thieving lot of Yanks over there could never produce a woman anywhere near worthy of an officer of Her Majesty's Northwest Mounted Police. They're bound to be ignorant trash in a place like that, and you'd be damn' well advised to. . . ."

For the first time in his life, Mac, stung beyond prudence, broke in on an officer's rebuke. Louder and sharper, he said: "They can't be too ignorant, sir, they've been taking a fortune in gold out of Canadian soil for over a year."

The colonel's mouth was suddenly paralyzed on the way to a question; it then worked futilely for a moment and finally managed the parade ground bark that had terrified subalterns for two decades: *"What?!"*

It was his utter faith in Callie's intelligence and rectitude that had brought Mac to this pass. He had no regrets, insisted firmly and much too loudly that he had been given a map, and insisted that the colonel should telegraph Ottawa for the results of the latest land survey if he doubted his word or, more importantly, "that of the woman I love."

The colonel's answer was in the form of a continuous bellow that resounded all over the post and made even the horses shudder.

"That laundry of yours is top of the barrel, Miss Callie," Jude Slocum said. "Got them coming in from all over the territory just to get clean. It's a wonderment."

Callie, taller somehow, direct in the way she looked at people, a presence in an attractive blue dress, white shawl, boots, and makeup, merely smiled; she had made it a rule never to discuss her success with anyone but Claude. It was satisfying that the last time she had seen Jude he had spoken above her head, now he looked into her face.

They were standing where there should have been a sidewalk, in the muddy street outside the best of the town's cafés.

"So how's the bank doing, Emmett? Unusual color, I have to say, but eye-catching. Good sign out front, too. By golly, the two of you look well turned out."

Claude, at Callie's insistence, all dressed up in a new suit and tie, a little self-conscious, tried to look serious and responsible. "We're in it for the long haul. We believe in the future." He looked to Callie to see if he had come up with the right bromides. "What's short are depositors and borrowers. The business climate isn't real good right now."

Jude nodded. "We all got problems these days, don't let it get you down." He turned to Callie with a grin. "Talks just like a business man, too, doesn't he?"

"We do, and we are," she told him bluntly, then teased with her *faux* innocent smile.

Jude, like most men, enjoyed it. "I believe you are."

Claude drew himself up. This being respectable wasn't so bad, and Callie beamed at him.

"Come on in and meet some of your fellow business men. Those who are left. We're having a little meeting about the state of our town."

Across the street, some of Satan's darker angels observed the trio from a bench in the shadows of the livery stable where they sat handing a bottle of rye whisky back and forth.

"High on the hog, ain't they?" fat Billy said to his brother. "What good is it, I'm askin' you, us bein' Swopes? Livin' on pickin's. You got any more money, by the by?"

Jorem didn't deign to answer. "I tell you one thing. I'm sick to my stomach o' bein' beat on by Daddy and bossed around by Tom and ol' stupid McNab."

"What we gonna do 'bout it?"

"Hell, you don't git beat, whatta you care?"

"I git teased, an' all the shitty jobs there is."

"Let's you and me git the hell outta here, Brother," Jorem decided.

"Where 'bouts?"

"I don' know. Dawson, Juneau, Skagway, maybe all the way home. How'd you like that, huh, see Zion again, Billy?"

"How? We don't have a pot to piss in."

Just then, in one of those fatal happenstances that direct

the attention of malign gods to the affairs of unwary humans, there was bright laughter across the street. Callie's laugh in particular was striking.

Looking over there again, the two Swopes saw Jude put his arms around the shoulders of Callie and Claude, guiding them into the restaurant. It was enough to spark tinder in slow minds.

"They do," Jorem said, more to himself.

In the office at the back of the bank, he stood first on one foot and then the other, like someone aching to relieve himself. "You fat peckerhead. Hurry it up or we're cooked."

"I only done this oncet afore, Jorem. In Coeur d'Alene, I think it was. Only feller was forewarned, and all we found was a safe full of his dirty socks. We was so burnt by a low trick like that, we blowed up the building instead." He stopped to visualize that lovely moment of his life. "You should 'a' seen it go."

"Jist shut up, Billy, and git to work, or, I swear, I'll settle you myself." He drew his pistol and began spinning it on his finger.

A cold north wind had come down off the high country but did nothing to hurry Callie and Claude, his arm around her, back to the boarding house.

"Let's go *now*. You made a pile already, and I got plenty. Winter's coming. It's not like down there, nothing like what you're used to. Man can freeze to death in a few minutes."

"You forget, I got a debt to pay."

"You already sent that church more money than's good for pious people."

"Isn't the debt I mean."

He stopped them, yet even from inches away couldn't bring himself to look her in the eye, but ended up studying the mud on his boots. "Callie, would you think maybe . . . of marrying me?"

She looked at him in amazement for a second while he squirmed in place like a fifteen-year-old. "Claude Emmett, have you lost your senses? Do you realize what you just said?"

"Look at me, I'm respectable, God help me . . . the wild rover no more."

"It suits you," she said, smiling, "but the answer is no."

"Why? Is it Mac? That fool redcoat? I just refuse to believe. . . ."

"No! Not necessarily. I just can't seem to make up my mind what I want."

"That's no reason," he complained, before grabbing and kissing her. Not only did she fail to resist, but she kissed him back. The *boom* that came from two blocks away scarcely made a dent in all this bliss.

Callie pulled back. "What's that?"

"My mind exploded," he said, and kissed her again, the two of them standing there in the mud, oblivious of that early Arctic wind whistling through. Even Claude's hat being cart-wheeled down the street went unnoticed.

Smoke was still coming from the safe and a sulphur-like odor filled the room. Jorem and Billy coughed, but, otherwise, they didn't care, didn't care about anything, even getting caught, so enamored were they of what they had found.

"Hallelujah!" Jorem said, piling in with both hands.

"Judas Priest, look it! We're millionaires." Billy stopped to dig into some dust and let it fall back through his plump fingers.

They were dragging bags of dust and nuggets, almost all of it Claude's hard-earned take from trail robberies, out of the safe and dumping it into a potato sack.

"Jist hold it still, dumb-ass."

With a canvas money bag right in front of him, Jorem noticed something. "Whoooa, brother. There's sump'in' I don't git. . . ."

"I thought we was hurryin'."

"Look here." He held the corner up close to Billy's face.

"Huh?"

"That little mark in the corner you can hardly see. Don't that look to you like Daddy's lodge sign he uses to mark our gold?" Alerted, he looked past his brother's head at the safe. "What's that other in there?"

Billy turned and reached in. "Ain't nothin'. Jist a raggedy old parka." He pulled it out and held it up for display. "It's jist like them damn' socks again."

"That parka's blue-colored, Billy. Blue. Don't you know . . . that guard I took his yeller boots from when we hung 'im claimed it was the Blue Parka Man robbed 'em, only Daddy figured he was lyin'. He weren't. This feller here ain't no banker." He let out a rodeo yell that drove the remaining smoke out of the room.

"Jorem, don't . . . ! I don't like this, Brother, it scares me." Billy's face brightened with a better idea. "I know! We could leave Daddy a note."

Jorem, like his brother, bore the mark, if not quite so much of the strain, of thinking upon his brow. "No, we ain't goin' now. What we're gonna do is make Daddy love us best."

Chapter Nineteen

A few people came out on the street with coats and wraps over their nightclothes or underwear in answer to their curiosity about the *boom,* which in turn put an end to any kissing. Someone mentioned to Claude that it sounded as if it might have come from his bank. He had sensed that all along, but his libido had refused it admission to the left hemisphere.

There was no one inside, and, when they went through into his office, the only window in the back wall of the building was wide open. The safe door hung askew on one hinge, its combination dial shattered. There was the open potato sack and a lot of gold dust scattered on the floor, plus the pungent odor of exploded dynamite.

"Oh, dear Lord," Callie said. "What did they get, Claude?"

Kneeling, he poked around inside, examining it with the help of an oil lamp handed him by Callie. "Not much. What the devil! Something peculiar here . . ."

In the courthouse/saloon a single bag of gold nuggets lay spilling its guts across a card table in front of John Brown Swope. The canvas corner bearing the Masonic sign was held high over it, framed by Jorem's dirty fingers. On the felt beside the gold lay the parka, looking like a crumpled man on a green lawn.

The boys were rattling on with a lame tale of how a complete stranger in town had blown the safe and they had rushed in to apprehend him, only to find the evidence that now sat before him.

The head of the clan wasn't listening. John Brown broke in on them, poking the one bag. "Is this all was in there?"

"Heck no, Daddy," Jorem reassured him, "there was a fortune in there. That Emmett must 'a' stole millions."

"Where is it now?" How could a voice become as cold as space and yet have the feel and smell of burning flesh? The old man's eyebrows saluted heaven at the corners.

"Uhm . . . we left it," Jorem said. He knew it was up to him because Billy had begun making tiny squeaks, as if trying to find a voice that wasn't there. "We knowed how you liked things to look legal and all, an' we figured after you hung 'im. . . ."

They should have known it was coming, they had seen it often enough, but, when the old man slammed the table hard enough to break it, they both jumped back.

"No man born of woman ever made a fool of me and had the privilege of going on living on God's good green earth. They will be devoured by the hounds of hell. I will crucify them and mount their heads on pikes on the main street of this town. So saith the prophet of the Lord God Jehovah!"

Excitement over, the small crowd attracted by the explosion had returned to the comparative safety of their beds. Claude and Callie sat in the office. She had his swivel chair, and he was in the padded guest's chair—both brought a great distance at considerable cost. A lantern atop the oak desk cast a pale red glow on both their faces, showing the concern to be found there. It shared its light with a bottle of Scotch whisky, an ashtray, two bags of nuggets, and the soles of four boots. Both were smoking quality cigars.

"No matter how I twist and turn it, it's like one of those

damn' kaleidoscopes, keeps shifting in my mind. Doesn't figure, only one bag of gold. Leaving a hundred thousand. Rough count."

"Maybe," Callie speculated, "we scared them. Or something did."

"Thieves we got around here seeing that much gold would have shot it out with the U.S. cavalry before they'd give it up."

"Desperate miner? Took only what he needed?"

"Know anybody like that, do you? And why'd they take my parka?"

Callie sat up and put her drink down hard on the desk. "You kept your parka in there? The *blue parka?!*"

"I'm sentimental."

"Oh, God, Claude!"

"I know." He suddenly stared ahead, squinting. "What's that?" Like Jorem before him, his attention had been drawn to one of the bags on the desk in front of him.

"What?" She leaned close and reached out for it. "What are you looking at?"

"That little mark in the corner." He pushed it closer to Callie.

Callie studied it for a minute. "That's a Masonic Lodge sign. Papa's a member, only they don't let him come to meetings." Her voice dipped low with suspicion. "Where did you get this bag?"

"Came off a gold train going down to Skagway." Grinning with pride, he sat back again and locked his hands behind his head. "Took the whole damn' thing, four mules' worth, without firing a shot. I tell you, honey, it was a thing of beauty, like a famous painting. I'm the Whistler of trail robbers."

"And who owned this gold?"

His grin broadened quickly—"Swopes."—then faded slowly under her relentless gaze.

"That man hanging when we first came into town? Someone said he'd lost them a lot of gold in a robbery."

"Uhm. . . ." He nodded reluctantly.

"You've just been robbed by someone who took only one bag of gold because they found something far more important . . . your parka. And sure as God made little green apples, the Swopes know right now who stole their gold. All hundred of them."

"You're not cheering me up any."

Even Callie's tone turned despairing. "Claude, how did you ever survive this long?"

He rubbed his head. "I dunno. Respectability's made me stupid, seems like."

Callie, too, sat back but could merely sigh. Should they stay and bluff it out or flee before the night was over? How would they get the gold out at this hour and then expect to survive on the trail, moving ponderously out in the open? More importantly, how long did they have? As it turned out, not long.

A pounding at the front door brought them both to attention. Claude came around the desk. The Navy Colt was in the drawer, once again a part of his life.

He told Callie to stay where she was and went out of the office. In a moment he returned with an agitated Jude Slocum and the storekeeper, Bob Fairly. When the three of them bustled into the office, they found themselves confronting Callie with Claude's .38 pointed squarely at their midsections.

The men gasped, but she said a soft—"Gentlemen."—and put it down atop a cabinet behind the desk.

Jude shook his head; this woman's spirit never ceased to

amaze him. He had no illusions, but he had begun to feel a powerful attraction. *A little late,* he thought.

Fairly, breathless, stammered: "There's a warrant on you. Swopes all around the courthouse right now, with more coming in." To Callie, he said: "Already been over to your rooming house."

"Can we get horses?" she asked.

Claude looked off and gave it only an instant's thought. "God dammit, I'm not going!" Spinning back to her, he softened: "But you sure are. Jude, can you give her one or find one?" Without waiting for an answer, he made a gesture as if to hand her over to Slocum. "See her out of here, would you?"

She pulled away from Jude's attempt to become her escort and planted her feet. "Half an hour ago you wanted me to elope with you, or whatever that was, ride right out of town la-de-da like a couple of Gypsies with whatever we could carry and just keep going."

"I changed my mind. Before, all I thought about was getting you alone somewhere and raiding your bloomers. I was willing to give up a god-damn' fortune for that, so you ought to be flattered."

She spat at him—"Well, I'm not!"—but at the same time blushed, sensing how ridiculous it was under these circumstances.

"Maybe you two should have this little imbroglio some other time," Slocum suggested sharply, looking through the door to the front.

Claude gave no sign of having heard him, and went right on: "Callie, the god-damn' sons-of-bitches want to take my respectability away from me. Banker Emmett! I like that. It's the god-damn' principle of the thing. Besides, I hate 'em."

"Well, if you're fool enough to stay, so am I."

"No, you're not. . . ."

More timidly, Fairly said: "We just come to warn you. You don't have much time."

"Neither do we," Slocum said. "I think I saw something. Across the street."

"You can open another bank, Claude, somewhere sane!"

A fusillade of shots came and the sound of the big picture window in front being shattered, glass raining everywhere.

Claude cried out in pain: "My window! My damn' plate glass window from Seattle." At the same time he had the presence of mind to blow out the single lantern on the desk.

"I'd say that ends the lovey-dovey or noble sentiments or whatever those were," Slocum said acidulously. "The Swopes brought a damn' army down on us. You got any guns around here?" He already had a small pistol in his hand.

"You can still get out the back," Claude said. "I'll show a white flag and tell 'em."

"Naw, too late."

Fairly, beside him, was quivering. "Whatta we gonna do?"

"I don't know what you're gonna do, Bob, but you've been in the forefront talkin' about runnin' the Swopes out of here, remember? Now's your chance."

"Jude, we got *no* chance. Against all them out there? There's hundreds. They'll skin us alive."

"You might try surrendering to them," Slocum advised Claude. "See what that gets you."

Claude had flung open a closet where he kept a modest gun cabinet. For himself, another Colt. For Callie, he extracted her venerable shotgun. Ammunition was handed around freely. Slocum chose a Winchester and threw an old carbine at Fairly.

The latter took it as if it were an overripe cheese. "I was going to send to Montana for my wife any day now." Another burst of gunfire out on the streets sent him ducking behind Claude's desk. "Oh, Lordy. Oh, Lordy. . . ."

Everyone was down behind something or huddled in a corner, not knowing where the next attack would come from.

"I don't mean to embarrass anybody," Callie said in a shaky voice, "but I'm going to say a short prayer here."

"Hell," Claude said, peering out into the dark, "get us all into it. And while you're praying, you and God keep your eye out that back window."

He led the men in easing out into the bank proper, sidewinding on their bellies. Shots came in sporadically, seemingly without special purpose, but people could be seen running in and out of buildings and on the streets in both directions. Puffs of smoke came from windows and doorways, looking almost gentle. Little chips of wood flew about; glass broke and fell; the sound of men shouting to each other in all directions; dogs barking and horses neighing. President McKinley's picture fell off the wall. It was not encouraging.

"Sure make a lot of noise, don't they?" Slocum said.

The three spread out, staying behind the heavy wooden counters of the tellers' cages.

"Their first mistake . . . should've come right at us through the door," Claude said.

Callie was outraged by the illegality. "They didn't even try to serve the warrant," she called from the back.

"I think these shots, here," Slocum said, "are just to keep our heads down. There'll be more of 'em coming along."

"Anyone around here gonna show up to help us?" Claude asked him.

"Only if we're winning."

Claude grunted. It was what he had expected.

Fairly was defensive. "Lot of them are family men, like me."

"I don't recollect I ever heard you mention your family before, Bob," Slocum said.

Claude broke open and checked the chambers on both of his pistols, hefted the one in his left hand several times to get the feel. He wasn't much good with that hand, but, using both, he could put up a volume of fire. His stomach felt like the pit of a volcano, and he almost resented Slocum his apparent calm. Here he was, just a local business man and with practically no stake in all this, risking his life with them. It was unnatural.

Even now, Slocum, still wearing his derby, crawled across the floor of the bank to the front, hiding himself in a corner where he could see down the street to his right through the marginal glass remaining in the large window. The only way he could see in the other direction, to his left, would have been to break away the glass, which he did with the butt of the Winchester, and crane his head out and around, turning it into the target equivalent of a watermelon on a pole. He settled for firing off a few rounds at the blacksmith's almost directly across the street, silencing a gunman hidden there.

From the office door, Callie said: "Claude, someone has to go to Mac for help."

"How's he gonna help us? He's one man . . . not even an American," Claude argued, and then was forced to bury his face in the dust of the floor when a volley came in through the destroyed window, several rounds *thunking* into the counter.

"There's no one else," she said, and crawled back to her

posting at the rear window, putting an end to the night-out taffeta dress.

Claude decided that, even if it was the logic of despair, hers was irrefutable. He asked Fairly if he was willing to try to get out and ride to the Mountie post across the border?

The storekeeper responded eagerly: "I'll go. I will, I'll try. . . ."

The question was how to get him outside safely? Slocum said he had a very fast horse in the stable. The three discussed the idea of a white flag, but nobody believed it would work.

The volume of incoming fire was increasing, so Claude crawled forward, cutting himself in several places on the scattered shards, to kick open the front door and position himself to fire though it. It also gave him a good view to the left which was Slocum's blind spot.

Claude suggested Fairly might still get out that back window as it was very dark out there, but that idea vanished with the crash of Callie's shotgun, followed by something that could have been her celebrating or crying out in agony.

Claude, alarmed, shouted to her.

"I'm all right. Some of them were coming up to the window, saying things."

"You get 'em?"

"I don't know, but they're gone."

Somewhere in town a bugle was blown wildly, not anything they could recognize but its very indifference to musical norms giving it an eerie quality. Slocum seemed to hear something else and strained to look, finding something down the street that excited him.

"They're coming. They got a white flag. It's the old man himself, by George."

Claude took the risk and looked out of the door from

down low, twisting to see up the street. There came old man Swope, no coat and the usual black suit, the wind blowing his beard over his shoulders on both sides. He cradled a shotgun across his chest with a Bible clutched in one hand, marching at a steady cadence in front of two or three dozen men and a couple of women, some mounted, all armed to the teeth. The men on either side of him carried torches. It had a certain majesty to it, Claude had to admit.

With the flash of an idea, he spoke sharply to Fairly: "Now, Bob! Now's the time. They won't risk our shooting the old man."

"Yes, I'll do it, now . . . now . . . ," the storekeeper said, breathless, encouraging himself. Ripping off his parka, he pulled his white shirt out of his pants and over his head, yanked the parka back on—the whole process taking less than thirty seconds.

"Sergeant MacDonald, remember. No one else," Claude coached.

"I'll remember. I will. . . ." He seemed ready to fall apart, with his head down so far he couldn't see where he was going and mouth dragging open as he slid toward the door.

"Go on!" Slocum shouted at him. "Git, god dammit, Bob!" From his prone position he tried to kick the man into action.

Fairly stumbled to his feet, waving his shirt around in the air as if it was a rallying point, plunged out the door and into the middle of the street. For a moment he gyrated crazily, still flourishing the white flag, disoriented, and trying to figure out which way led to the stable.

Possibly he presented such a bizarre apparition that no one would have fired at him anyway for a few moments, but, when he did finally take off, it was at a speed that should have worn his feet to nubs. Also it was in the opposite direction of the Swope posse's coming, where all eyes were focused.

With an upraised hand, the torches reflecting off his formidable peaks and crags, John Brown stopped the parade in the middle of the street although not quite opposite the bank. He raised a megaphone and showed it to let everyone know a pronouncement was coming.

Inside, Slocum itched to pot the old man right then and there. "Best chance we got."

"That what a business man would do?"

"Sure as hell. What do you think business is?"

"Well, I'm a trail robber, and we got our honor, and that's a white flag out there."

The venerable Swope's voice made the fragments of glass still imbedded in the window frame tinkle like wind chimes.

"Claude Emmett! I have here a warrant, signed by me as Third District Court Judge in the Territory of Alaska, for your apprehension and trial as the notorious bandit and murderer known as the 'Blue Parka Man.' The woman with you is your whore and accomplice. Anyone else inside, whoever they may be, is also an accomplice subject to the same penalties. Now hand yourselves over for judgment."

"Why would I do that?" Claude shouted.

John Brown pointed that forefinger dramatically, the one borrowed from the Sistine ceiling. "We shall be merciless if you resist."

Claude felt a presence beside him and realized it was Callie. "Who the hell's watching the back?" he whispered for no sensible reason.

"I closed the shutter. I wanted to see what was happening."

There was no time to argue it; he owed Swope an answer. "You'll be that anyway!" he yelled out the door.

"Say your prayers," Swope told them in that rolling *profundo* as a sort of benediction of doom. He started to leave the street at the same stately pace at which he had arrived.

Claude couldn't resist and called again: "They'll be saying 'em over you, old man, 'less you're off that street in five seconds."

The beleaguered experienced what was perhaps the last joy left to them in seeing the normally fire-breathing patriarch crank up his huge ancient body to hop, skip, and jump to cover, along with the rest of his tribe, looking like grasshoppers in a burning field. The street was empty in four seconds. Claude, Callie, and Slocum laughed, but not too hard.

Afterwards, in anticipation of a full-out frontal assault, Claude went back into his office and used some leftover building materials plus his desk to close up the single window. Slocum was worried about how it would leave the back of the building vulnerable to arson, but Claude argued that, particularly considering the current winds, even the Swopes must realize how the slightest conflagration could immediately involve the entire town. It was one of the great, wholly justified, fears of the Northwest.

A period of relative quiet followed. Claude leaned close to Callie. "If I thought they'd leave you alone, I'd go out there."

"You would, but they wouldn't. I never killed a man before, Claude." After a moment she was compelled to add: "And I'm still scared sick."

"Me, too. But I'll tell you what you're gonna do. We'll be taking a rush against us pretty soon. Get behind that cashier's cage, right in the middle with that shotgun. Keep your loads right next to you, and, when you see anyone in front of the bank, you give 'em one barrel. Any left standing, when the smoke clears, you give 'em the other. Don't think of it as killing, think of it as . . . well, don't think. All right, sweetheart?"

She showed a faint smile. "That sounds funny . . . 'sweetheart.' But nice."

He noted how her hand shook and held up his own for their mutual inspection. It, too, quivered, so he took hers in his, and they shook together, which gave them both a reassuring laugh. "I worked in a carnival once, and they called it stage fright. Believe me, once this thing starts, you won't have time for it. Now . . . lay the barrel on the counter and just aim, don't think. Reload as fast as you can, but don't burn yourself. When you crank it open, sometimes you want to blow out the barrel. Now get back there." He gave her hand a squeeze, then her person a little shove, calling to Slocum softly: "I figure they'll come charging over here now they got the men and the old man's watching. What do you think?"

"They're dumb as moose, why not?"

"I hope so."

Claude consulted his pocket watch—five after one. The wind was blowing black clouds across the sky that kept it darker than usual. Still, there was occasional moonlight for targeting.

When Bob Fairly catapulted himself out of the bank, he had every intention of becoming a real hero by riding madly for help. Unfortunately he was not the sort to embrace "madly" in any arena of his life. First, he tore down that street and dove into the stable, even though there was no pursuit. The smell of the horses and mules, the straw and leather, was so familiar, so normal, it acted to calm him immediately. He needed a moment to rest and sank down on the floor.

Shivering, he huddled into some straw. It was snug and warm. Bob began to feel safer than he had in a long time even though there were shots and angry shouts and death within earshot.

He began unconsciously to pull more straw in over him. In its embrace, his breathing became deep and steady. The cold sweat gradually evaporated from his forehead, relaxing his whole body. The sense of being so separate from all that chaos and horrible death down there made the other end of town the other side of the planet and brought an odd conviction of his own innocence. Sleep came easily.

Chapter Twenty

There had been only a few shots fired at the bank in the last half hour, but the defenders could feel the buildup to some kind of action like something carried on the air. Not only were they conserving their own ammunition, but they wanted to encourage a misapprehension on the part of the enemy. The greatest danger for them lay in attrition; they needed the risk of an all-out charge.

At last, a lantern bobbed frantically in the window of the barbershop across and to their left, and was repeated in the mortuary, the blacksmith's, and up and down the street.

"I imagine this just might be it," Claude said as casually as he could manage.

Almost on cue, shouts, yelps, and cries like an Indian uprising came from all around them in the gloom. The boys were whipping up their courage. Not a pleasant sound.

Then they burst out of doors, windows, and from between buildings, shooting from the hip, advancing with bravado.

"God forgive me," Callie said, looking along the barrels.

"Come on you sons-of-bitches," Slocum yelled to encourage himself, and raised his Winchester.

They waited until the charging men had taken a few steps into the street proper before opening up. Claude went to one knee, firing first with one gun and then the other. Even with pistols it was point-blank. They were shooting into both flanks and scoring. It would have been difficult to do otherwise the way the attackers were bunched up, but there were so many, they hardly noticed their losses and plowed ahead. Callie had not yet fired the scatter-gun.

It was as unlikely an army as ever seen, in derbies, one top hat, in felt and Western hats, miners' caps with ear flaps, although there wasn't a real miner among them, dressed for city, plowing, mining, Wild West, or tundra, and with every kind of weapon—hatchets, knives, cavalry rifles, handguns, shotguns. In their numbers and with the near-dark it was impossible to sort out individuals.

One particular fool rode out on a horse, and a bigger fool on a mule. The horse's rider tried to act out the rôle of a cowboy on a tear, digging in his spurs, probably the only pair in Alaska, while wahooing, waving on the rest with his hat and firing his six-shooter all over the place. All this presumably in imitation of the mythical West he had missed.

The horse shied from all the noise and confusion, reared, and dumped its rider into the churning street. Jorem, with a sprained ankle and wrist, was later to shoot it in revenge, never understanding how in its animal fear it had saved his life. All he knew was that he had been made to crawl back to cover, bruised and humiliated, through the mud and a forest of legs.

Slocum shot the mule in the head. It keeled over on its apparently drunken rider, pinning his leg to the ground. The man struggled to get free, but Slocum knew he could afford to leave him there for the moment and come back to kill him when he had more time. The main charge got right to the big empty window.

Callie still hadn't fired, although by now Claude was screaming at her to join the fight. He had emptied both of his guns and was reloading with trembling fingers, racing against having to hand-to-hand with a dozen berserkers intent on nothing else but killing him.

On the other side of the room, Slocum started to reload his Winchester, but decided he would never get it done in time, so stood and drew his pistol. A huge, red-headed man, his face streaked with Indian war paint and wielding a Civil War sword in one hand and a pistol in the other, was three feet away when he fired twice into his head. The man fell over the window sill at his feet, splattering blood on his assailant. Slocum retreated a few paces in revulsion, but he recovered quickly and leaped forward again to grab up the Winchester by the barrel and use it as a war club.

When the next attacker, brandishing an axe wildly over his head, his face covered with dirt, sweat, and blood that allowed only two bulging red eyes to glow through the mess, reached the window sill in the center and prepared to leap into the room, Callie at last overcame her panic and scruples, closed her eyes, and let fly with both barrels.

The dense spread of Double-0 at that range scythed like shrapnel through the first rank where they were bunched up to plunge inside, decimating it, and drove back the ones crowding up behind. The attack stalled, and then with a chorus of howls, screeches, and bellowed pleas and commands from across the street, staggered back, some able-bodied gunman supporting less fortunate comrades.

Both Claude and Slocum, exhausted, sick of the slaughter, let them go. In their wake, somewhat obscured by the clouds of wind-blown smoke that still clung to the ground, as if reluctant to leave their one battlefield seven dead or dying men and one mule—his rider had slipped out and away—lay on the muddy street where the pools of blood were large enough to reflect a sticky red moon between clouds.

There was some groaning and whimpering, but it was difficult to tell from where it came, the enemy was so close across the street. Soon there were added curses, threats, recriminations, and even the lamentations of the women. Callie cried softly at the sight of the mangled corpses piled up just outside and the one draped partially over the window sill. Slocum moved to push the remains of the redheaded giant outside.

"I think we killed Goliath," he murmured.

Claude looked down and realized that he had been shot in his left thigh, but as yet there was no pain. Slocum called over that he had just figured out that he had been struck in a rib, but it had obviously bounced off and he didn't think it was serious. Just a little stiffening on that side; he could still stand and shoot.

Claude went back to the office for the whisky bottle, stopping on the way to see if Callie was recovered. She responded weakly but definitively that she would be ready to do the same again, had already reloaded her gun, and only wanted a few minutes to herself. Claude gave her a quick hug, told her she had saved all their lives, and they would, somehow, get out of this, and remember this night. For the moment, at least, they should feel triumphant.

He doused his thigh with whisky and slid the bottle over to Slocum. As soon as the two had patched themselves up, they set to work by dragging what remained of the office furniture to build a barrier across the huge vacant window and doorway. It was decided that Callie should come forward and hold the center of this new fortification, that she should stay beneath it as in a trench during any exchange of gunfire, and only come up to fire at a signal from Claude.

At the moment only an occasional round came in, and most, for some reason, were aimed too high.

"You think it's like this for Mister Roosevelt and his Rough Riders down there in Cuba?" Callie said.

"When they come, will they come at us like that again?" Slocum wondered aloud.

Callie asked: "Would you slide that whisky over here."

"You hurt?" Claude asked, trying to keep his concern about her on a war footing.

The bottle traveled through a lot of broken glass and débris, but it got to her. "No, I'm not hurt."

"You sure?"

"Damn that's good," she said, having taken a hearty swig of the whisky.

Claude sighed. "Wouldn't you know, I finally loosened your stays, and it's too late to enjoy it."

"Day late and a dollar short," she allowed.

A light appeared in the shot-out window of one of the buildings a few doors up the street, and Slocum took a shot at it. It disappeared.

"I wish to hell we knew what was going on over there," Claude said, straining to see through the pale darkness.

The answer lay in the converted parlor of the sometime fortune-teller, full-time opium seller who was also the town's full-time mortician. Pronounced over an ancient brocaded couch from which stuffing escaped in handfuls at the corners: ". . . These children of Lucifer, these sons and daughters of whores, have laid low your obedient servant, McNab Elijah Clanton Swope, while in the righteous pursuit of Your work here on earth. We will send them to Thee for punishment, O Lord, knowing well Thou will commit them to the everlasting fires of hell, and other torments too terrible to recite before our womenfolk. His brothers will see to it before another sun has risen. Amen."

This was followed by a loud murmur of "Amen" from forty or so throats, all that could be crammed into the little room and others adjacent. John Brown remained on his knees before his stretched-out, marble-textured, increasingly blue-green son whose arms were folded over a Bible. His boots were at his feet and a candle on the end table at his head.

They had wiped free most of the blood that was on McNab's back, hands, and the front of the neck where there was an exit wound, but there had been no time to get him into his Sunday suit. As a result, the corpse still wore a holster and pistol.

After a prayerful silence, the old man, without rising or even looking around, said: "I find out the fool did this, I will kill him with these two hands." He held them up.

McNab, who had never heard of Stonewall Jackson, had, at the end of his life, shared with that estimable general a singular death—from friendly fire. The sons and daughters of whores across the street had put two rounds into his appendages, but that would never have been enough to stop what John Brown called his "Swope lion's heart." It was that one the devil had directed into the back of his neck that had settled him, while he, true Son of Dan, maintained his front to the enemy.

John Brown stood and turned around, whereupon everyone in the room found somewhere else to look, most with their heads supposedly down again in prayer. "Anyone found Tom?" he asked in a more reasonable voice only tinged with madness.

No one answered. Someone coughed nervously. It took Billy, who often said the unsayable simply because he understood neither the import nor consequences, to tell the truth. "Cousin Millie said she seen him ridin' south outta town with that lady o' easy virtue he was stuck on, you know . . . Belle? Ding-Dong Belle?" He snickered.

"No," John Brown said, still quietly, while his face

turned to burning pitch, "I didn't know. Nobody told me, neither. I warned the boy. . . ."

"Oh, yeah, he packed up lickety-split minute you 'nounced the posse. Rode outta here like demons was after 'im."

"Everybody begone!" the old man ordered abruptly. "Everybody except my sons."

People tended to step lively at that, but he didn't wait before he turned on the two remaining boys.

"Your brother lies dead," he said, indicating McNab behind him. "Died in a way no father could regret. Pride is all I feel. Pride. Yet another's run off with a whore. My second-born a coward. A whoremonger and a deserter. I will not hesitate to execute this deserter as any other, and God will forgive me."

Both boys began instinctively to edge away, some of the horror of the situation beginning to seep through Billy's brain barrier.

The old man pointed again to McNab. "Go and kiss your brother."

"Huh?" Jorem said.

Billy shuddered. "Do we have to?"

"Kiss your brother and swear to Almighty God by his soul and your own that you will slay the ones who did that to him this very night."

"I thought it was one of us shot him in the back," Billy whined. He did not enjoy corpse-kissing.

The old man looked at him with such contempt he felt his penis wither.

"They who *caused* him to die. Swear it, and then kiss that noble young man."

They swore, and stepped over quickly to kiss the corpse on its hard blue lips, afraid to fake it. Billy disguised the fact that he wiped his lips with a handkerchief immediately afterwards.

"You are my only remaining sons. May the Lord strengthen your arm as you go to smite the murderers of your race."

The boys looked at each other in awe; their father finally wanted them, needed them. It was almost as if God was sending them forth to kill under his auspice the people they hated most in the world. It was a feeling almost holy.

Someone fired a quick dozen rounds into the bank, spreading them around and causing the defenders to put their mouths and noses to the floor. Slocum cried out, and the other two were frantic to find out how he fared.

"I'm all right. I'm all right. Caught me in my foot. I gotta take off my boot here and see . . . but I think I can still get up, if I hold onto the wall. I need some more bandages."

Callie ripped into her dress and crawled over to hand it to him. She wanted to put the bandage on him, but he told her to get back to her scatter-gun. Even in the gloom she could see him pouring blood out of his boot.

"How long you figure we got?" he asked, his voice weaker than before.

Claude said—"Long as the whisky lasts."—and everyone tried to laugh at that.

Within a few minutes, another bullet singed Claude's face on the left side by the cheek bone. It burned and bled, but he, too, reported that he could still fight. The extent of Callie's damage was two bullets through her dress and a few glass cuts and bruises.

Slocum thought: "We probably got till dawn when they'll be able to see better."

They talked because it wasn't a time to feel yourself

alone. Death loves company.

"Oh, damn," Callie said, returning from the privy.

"What?" Claude asked, concerned.

"I've got the curse."

The men started to laugh, and it went on for several minutes, the absurdity of it refusing to let go of them, until, eventually, Callie joined in and the three of them howled. It made good propaganda across the way.

While they were winding down, something hit the back wall in Claude's office. All three stopped to listen.

"Somebody doesn't want to wait," Callie said softly.

Outside in back, Jorem and Billy were trying to lasso anything on the flat roof that would support their weight, and as quietly as possible. They were keen, in good spirits, having consumed a lot of liquor, but on a mission.

The rope caught finally on a small metal chimney used for the Franklin stove inside. Jorem tried it, and it seemed to support him. "Lemme go first, you're too fat and it might break."

He had his pistol in the holster, a hatchet in his belt, and a shotgun strapped on his back. His idea was to find an opening, chop one open if he had to, and rain pellets on the exposed defenders below who would have nowhere to hide. A strong young man, he started up the rope, hand over hand, using his feet against the back wall of the bank, leading to the inevitable *thunks*.

"I'll go up on the roof," Claude told the others, when even drawing himself to a standing position was agony.

Callie argued that she was the only one unwounded, but he insisted it was his bank, his fault they were in this, and it was not the sort of a situation that called for a woman with a shotgun as big as she was. Anyway, he was already on his way.

There was a storeroom in the back, containing all the paper products and records, and also a ladder to an opening on the roof. The wound on his face didn't bother him much, that was just pain, a burning sensation, but the thigh had stiffened and hurt hideously. Still, he managed to drag himself to the ladder and begin an ascent. With movement he loosened up a little. It was necessary to climb mostly with one hand while the other held the Colt in an upright position just in case he met the enemy coming down.

The only sound now, aside from an occasional gunshot, was his own breathing. Easing open the trap door at the top, he cocked an ear and listened through the slit. The first thing heard was a cat meowing. Then, at some remove, Billy's voice in a loudly whispered plea: "Jorem! Jorem! Help me, damn your eyes. . . ." Seemingly it came from the back wall.

Easing the lid wider, Claude looked around for the cat. It was a scruffy old tom that had come with the building and been fed by Claude and the workers at the laundry next door. There were a few snowflakes blowing in, but nothing that stayed on the ground. The roof itself was flat with a low wooden wall around it and a large water tank in the center. Presumably the cat was somewhere behind that. Billy sounded as though he could still be on the ground behind the building. Where was Jorem? Claude's best guess was, also back there on the ground where his brother was in some sort of difficulty.

He dragged himself up onto the roof and closed the trap door gently. There seemed so much light up here, and dawn was threatening in the east. Looking to the back, he could see where the rope had fixed itself to the little chimney and trailed back over the edge the roof.

Crawling closer, he could mark the strain on the rope,

see it tremble. Someone was on the way up. He drew in air quietly so that he wouldn't have to breathe, slipped off his boots, and wriggled toward it, hoping to intercept them, however many they were, at their most vulnerable moment.

"Jorem!" Billy called again, sounding as if he were gargling.

His brother was already on the roof behind the tank and in a perfect position to shoot Claude in the back, if he looked over the side. But then he did what we all do, answered to the call of his character. Furious, sure that the cat's mewling would reveal his presence, he gave it a kick. Of course, the cat yowled as it flew out into the open.

Claude didn't have to see the cat; his career choice had given him certain instincts; he instantly understood his own error in turning away from the tank before checking it out. Rolling several times, he ended on his back facing up at it.

Jorem couldn't help but hear his brother demanding to know what had happened, knew he had made a terrible mistake in forcing the action precipitously, and felt he had no choice but to go on the offensive, which was his natural temperament.

He wasn't exactly sure where he would find his enemy, but he leveled his pistol. Claude knew exactly where he would appear.

Angry, used to winning by intimidation, Jorem came roaring and trigger-happy. He fired his first shot even before he had spotted Claude. Claude's gun hand was rested at the elbow on the rooftop; his first shot hit Jorem in the groin.

The kid didn't seem to feel it, but, now that he had found his target, managed to shoot Claude in the left side. It was a through-and-through just above the hip and centimeters from where it would have guaranteed certain, slow death by sepsis.

Claude's second shot, fired almost simultaneously, went through Swope's right lung. Blood came from the chest and mouth. There was a moment's odd hiatus, both sides frozen, feeling the shock and surprise that comes with serious body trauma, and then the sense on Jorem's part that he was mortally wounded brought him to a slow descent toward the rooftop, crumpling accordion-like from the knees up. His gun hung loosely in his fingers, then slipped and clattered along the tar paper.

Forgetting his pain, his wounds, startlingly physical in the fugue of combat, Claude sprang to his feet and actually ran over to kick the gun away from Jorem's outstretched if immobile hand, then back to the point where the rope crested the rooftop.

Looking over, there was Billy almost to the top, his mouth open, gasping, blood on his hands, eyes wide with panic when he saw Claude's ruin of a face staring down from a couple of feet above. He had tied the rope under him in a crude sling that could be ratcheted up with less risk of falling back. Within arm's reach of his goal before running out of strength, he dangled.

All he could think of to do now was heave himself around helter-skelter, like an insect in a web, while trying to get his pistol out of his belt. He carried two, fumbled one, and helplessly watched it drop between his legs, then reached for the other.

Claude had a hard time killing him, but he did. Two shots, straight down into his shoulder to the heart and another in the head. It made Claude a little sick, but this was a Swope and a son, after all.

Something must have sent an ineffable message over the

town that this struggle was the apogee because, first, all gunfire stopped; there was silence; then the dogs began to bark, donkeys brayed, and voices came from across the street, faint, plaintive: "Jorem? Billy-boy?" In the distance two oblivious whores were fighting.

Callie's anxious query came up through the trap door, almost a wail articulating the name of her lover. Claude's answer was abrupt and harsh; he was all right, and she should get back to her post.

He went to kneel over Jorem, who fought to speak through lungs that whistled and bled. "Don't kill me, will you. Daddy'll pay you. We're, Billy an' me, we're his only sons left. Old man couldn't . . . go on livin'. . . . Please, don't. . . ."

Claude's face, caught in that defining brief moment between a cloudy night and cloudy dawn, was black with a streak of pink, but everywhere cold and unforgiving.

"For killing that old man. Trying to rape my girl. For everything else I don't know about, and being a Swope and an all around son-of-a-bitch." Claude fell into a coughing fit, totally unaware of the tide of blood spreading across his pants in front and back. "I hereby convene a miners' court and find you guilty. The sentence is death." He pointed his pistol. "May God have no mercy."

Something Jorem had said . . . an idea struck him that brought a pause. Callie would have to help; he was too weak to do it himself. Would she forgive him an act so gruesome? However extreme, however ugly, hope was fugitive, otherwise, and it might just save them, or at least one or two of them. . . .

Chapter Twenty-One

As the rising sun managed to break through in part, dogs came out in the chilly air to sniff at the corpses, looked around guiltily, unwilling to try their luck just yet. Buzzards circled just above the rooftops. Fortunately the cold retarded decay and suppressed odors.

Claude, whose recent wound had horrified Callie when she came up on the roof, was well-bandaged and back at his post by the door. She had poured the last of the whisky right through it and him. So weak was he, though, that it would have been almost impossible to move without help. Unconsciousness was a constant, nagging threat.

Slocum was a little better off, but so discouraged and debilitated that he had ceased to talk.

Callie, terribly worried about the men, was herself wide awake, posted in the middle where she kept the Smith & Wesson and even Claude's Derringer beside her as an adjunct to the shotgun. Something about this hideous night had steeled her, made her more determined to fight to the death. For the first time she realized how you could forgot even that you were human much less female.

On the other side, in what had been a whorehouse, several men of the Swope clan, all armed, were involved in an excited dialogue, when John Brown's favorite nephew—to the extent that he had a favorite anything—Levi, came into the room in answer to their summons. They led him to the large picture window of the parlor and parted the lace curtains.

Morning light crept through the rickety town, its streets an odd mixture of dust and mud from the previous night's mix of wind and snow. One corpse from the charge had just been pulled to cover by an intrepid boy, but most of the rest remained in all their grotesquerie. That wasn't why they had brought him, nor did it have anything to do with the enemy's stratagems. Within seconds he was racing for the funeral parlor next door.

Inside, he had to put a handkerchief over his face in order to go into the room where McNab was laid out. John Brown slept compressed like an accordion on a divan opposite the body. He shook his uncle awake.

"The boys come back yet? I couldn't stay awake any longer. Where are they?"

Levi merely shook his head, which was not unusual for him, and led his uncle into the next room where the old man dipped his hands into a basin of cold water, threw it into his face, and shook it off like a dog.

"Now, what is it?" There was a rare tinge of anxiety in the old man's voice.

Levi tilted his head to indicate direction, then led him to the door, and opened it cautiously. He pointed across and up. There, caught by the sun as it climbed the buildings, were Jorem and Billy Swope, hung at opposite ends of the same rope from the roof of the bank. Their pants were soiled by fear, eyes bulged, purple tongues seemed to have lunged out of their mouths and then fallen exhausted across the lips. The corpses were covered in their own blood and matter, already attracting black flies. The *buzzing* could be heard in the bank below.

John Brown stepped into the street and let out a cry so horrible and penetrating that it was heard through the entire town and stopped all movement. People ceased eating, talking, even having sex, which was always going on somewhere. Dogs ran along the street with their heads down.

In the bank, two of the three watched with the same sense of awe, with the same ice gripping the spine. One, who might be dying, felt differently. "You like to see people hang, you old bastard? See that!" Claude cried.

Swope staggered into the street, screaming—"My sons! My sons!"—and fell on his knees in his filthy black suit, still with a pistol stuck in his belt. He bowed his head in the dirt, sobbing and calling upon the Lord Jehovah to return them to "a father's loving embrace." He raised his head and tore at his beard, threw dirt into his face and on his head.

"Oh, Claude, what have we done?" Callie cried. When there was no reply, she forced herself to look up at the dangling legs as penance.

No one suggested shooting the old man. Swopes and their allies began to climb onto roofs or stand openly in doors and shattered windows, looking on, bewildered as children and as terrified as if Christ had returned and asked for a reckoning.

Only once did the old man address in his grief the killers of his boys, brandishing a fist at the bank while still on his knees and roaring Ahab-like: "I'll pursue your souls to hell and back!"

Claude, at least, believed him. "I'll be waiting!" he shouted back.

The moment passed, and back the old man went to the awful grief, tearing his clothes now, repeating—"My boys, my boys."—over and over. He began to lacerate his face, tearing hideous red streaks down across his cheeks, where the blood dripped off his tangled beard.

Callie could no longer look. She wouldn't have wished this on Papa.

John Brown lay a long time, stretched out in the street with his face down and arms spread wide, a crucifix in the Yukon filth. During that period nothing stirred but animals and wind that blew up occasional flurries of dust. Finally the old man rose to his full height, but if his people expected him to return to them, they were disappointed. He seemed unaware of his surroundings and lurched away up the empty street as if searching a desolated world for something lost. No one came near or even tried to speak to him.

"I guess it worked," Callie said. "What we did."

Claude had drifted off and had to shake himself awake. "What?"

"He seems broken."

"Maybe." He shook his head vigorously and when that wasn't enough, struck himself in the face, finally picked up a shard of glass and closed his fist on it.

Callie could see him now in the morning light and exclaimed at it. "Are you still bleeding, Claude?"

"I don't think so."

"Good. Then lay still, darling."

"Wish I had something to eat," he said, barely above a whisper.

"Soon. Do you want me to get you some water."

"Careful," was all he could manage to say.

"Think they'll send someone over, or just drift away?" Slocum asked.

Callie didn't answer, she was on her way back to the spigot at the sink next to the office. A couple of rounds had penetrated the water tank on the roof but, because of the angle, near the top. As a result, there was plenty left.

"I dunno," Claude answered him dully.

"Maybe I should go out there and find out," Slocum persisted.

"Not yet," Claude said, and dozed off.

"We can't last like this," Slocum said, but he remained where he was.

Another forty minutes went by without a sign of hostility or the return of the old man. Nothing out there. Across the street they were a little less careful, but remained inside or behind cover most of the time.

In the bank, both men dozed while Callie kept watch. She had not slept in thirty hours, but had lived the life of a warrior now and come to accept its hardships as normal, even in a taffeta dress. She was the only one unwounded; the job rightfully fell to her. Claude worried her the most; his wounds seemed far more dire. Besides, she loved him.

As the morning wore on, the wind slowed to a breeze, and it began to cloud up, darkening the landscape once more. She saw two little boys run out and drag in the corpses by the legs or arms. Their fathers or brothers or uncles, for all she knew. Clouds of flies rising off of them made her turn her head. The boys couldn't know who was watching them but seemed convinced that no one would shoot.

The street looked a little better after that, contributing to a growing optimism on her part. The men, too, felt it whenever they eased back into consciousness.

Slocum managed to stand, still half in cover, Callie sat up, showing part of her head over the barricade, and even Claude pulled himself up to a sitting position, suppressing a groan.

"No sign of anything," Callie said, straining to see up and down the empty street.

Slocum declared: "They've gone."

Claude was skeptical. "Where would they go?"

They went back to waiting. Finally even Callie was losing her ability to stay awake and function. She put her head down on her forearm. Whisky and passion had kept out the cold through the night, but no more.

Slocum shook himself alert and decided he had had enough. Without saying anything to his companions, he put his derby on his head, slung his Winchester under his arm, and stepped over the window sill onto the street. Claude and Callie were totally unaware.

He went a couple of steps farther out and turned to look back at the hanged men, registering his distaste. Then he turned and, almost jaunty, whistling "The Man Who Broke the Bank at Monte Carlo," walked in the footsteps of the old man toward the heart of town.

A barrage of shots, perhaps twenty, from all along the other side of the street broke the silence, knocked his legs out from under him, and killed him before he struck the ground.

Claude woke abruptly, yelling, and Callie, fuzzy herself, ducked lower for an instant, then came back up with her shotgun and began firing rapidly and systematically at the buildings, taking them in turn, yelling her fury at each. Claude, cursing, unloaded his gun, reloaded, and emptied it again, reloaded and . . . no thought given to conserving ammunition.

The fire from the other side slacked off, but Slocum's body still lay like old rags in the dust. His derby rolled back and forth nearby, buffeted by the breeze. Callie cried.

Now it was hopeless. Furthermore the enemy over there was completely unknown, faceless, without the old man and his lethal children. That made it worse somehow. Nothing remained but death at the hands of what must be the dregs of the Swope clan.

Exhaustion nipped at them like hot pincers, letting them drift off and jarring them painfully awake. They were both determined that, before they would be taken alive and made helpless, they would go out into the street, shooting.

"Don't fall asleep," Callie warned. "Maybe we should talk."

"You talk. I don't have it in me."

Neither spoke after that.

At noon Callie raised her head, dangerous now because the occasional round was coming in. "I thought I heard music?"

"Not likely."

She shivered and looked at the sky. "Could have a storm. Maybe the first snow."

"Won't hesitate to burn us out if that happens. 'Fact, I think I smell coal oil."

Callie started to say something, then hesitated. "That is music, Claude."

"That lunatic with the bugle last night." His voice devoid of hope or energy.

"No."

"Sweet Mother of God!" Claude tried to shout, "that's the charge." Now he felt the chill, and his whole body shook with emotion. As soon as he could fight the pain to a draw, he urged himself up to a standing position.

A thunder rolled in from the east, gunfire from heavy military rifles and pistols along with the loud clatter of a squadron of horse, coarse shouts, and panicked screams with a few *pop-pops* from other makes of weapons, echoing down the one long street. As a wave it swept closer in seconds.

When she saw the first Mountie, Callie leaped out into the street, jumping up and down and cheering at the top of her voice. Claude tried to tell her to be careful, but it was useless. He gave up and stumbled outside, limping badly, dripping some blood, holding onto his side. After her initial expression of joy, she ran to kneel beside Slocum, but there was no doubt their comrade was dead. She rose and looked back sadly at Claude, who was leaning against the side of the bank, to shake her head.

All around them, what seemed like hundreds of Mounties but actually numbering thirty-two were rooting out Swopes or their allies, firing from the saddle but satisfied in most cases merely to drive them out of town onto the trails, since there was so little real resistance.

The troop was composed mostly of that which had been at Fort McKenzie on a training exercise. Colonel Thursby, Mac in tow, had commandeered them when he received word back from Ottawa that the town of Daughton was, indeed, Canadian territory. Considering the reputation of the place, plus the sound of gunfire emanating from it, it was obvious to the colonel that it would be necessary to do more than show the flag in order to occupy it. A charge was called for; besides, he had never led one.

Everything had given way; the only obstacle being an obviously demented, filthy old man standing in the middle of the street, tearing out his hair and evoking God. The troop flowed around him.

Mac knew nothing of what had been happening with his friends; what brought his plunging horse to a stop was the spectacle of two young men hanging from a building. Only then did he look down and see Callie, who again screamed her joy at the sight of him. He shouted a greeting, laughed, and, casting off his usual reserve, rode over to reach down and pick her up, sweeping her onto his horse.

Claude looked on with that certain sad smile defeated

lovers show when they wish to demonstrate how they can receive heartbreak with grace and style. Anyway, he knew he was dying.

Callie said something to Mac, pointing to Claude, and he looked over, at the same time letting her slip back to the ground. He grinned at his old pard before recognizing the seriousness of his injuries, then leaped off his horse.

Before Mac could get to him, Claude suddenly paled as his blood pressure dropped like a plumb line, turned almost blue, opened his mouth in order to say something, but instead toppled heavily to the ground and lay face down without moving. Mac yelled, loud enough to tumble walls, for the company surgeon.

Bigger than Northfield, more entertaining than Coffeeville, The Great Bank Siege, as it would be remembered in the bars and brothels of Daughton for as long as the town existed, was over.

Epilogue

The Seattle station was overly busy late on an autumn afternoon with a number of trains stacked up, waiting to leave or come in and unload passengers. Part of the problem lay with the efforts of two electric mules to detach a posh car with gilt trimmings from one train and attach it to another that was impatiently spitting smoke and steam.

The three elderly occupants of the private coach strolled up and down the adjacent platform in a regal manner despite the hurly-burly all around them. They were so unaffected they appeared almost insubstantial, as if hurrying people might walk right through them without in any way disturbing their slow, elegant gait.

Passengers greeted or said sad good byes to families or friends; some raced for their trains, redcaps running behind with carts bearing so much luggage it blocked their vision. Conductors and crews banged on and poked at machinery, and waved things while shouting unintelligibly to everyone and no one. Great puffs of steam blew into people's faces, making them scamper, and reminding them that they were nothing compared to the mighty steel engines that knew every inch of this country.

A small group of shorn, scrubbed teenagers in sweaters, white bucks, and bobby-socks broke through or around the barriers and ran up and down the platform and even across the tracks, skipping, jumping, grinning obdurately, and holding their placards up to passenger car windows where bored, impatient travelers stared back without interest.

I LIKE IKE! REPUBLICAN YOUTH FOR A NEW AMERICA. HE WON THE WAR, HE'LL WIN THE PEACE. EISENHOWER IN FIFTY-TWO.

They came and went like lightning bugs in their young enthusiasm. The occupants of the private car never gave them so much as a look but continued on in their stately way, back and forth. People who had seen it all.

At a window seat on one of the waiting trains, held up just short of its destination, a fifty-year-old schoolteacher from Indianapolis was telling the hostess that this was her first trip to the West Coast, and, even though she was here to care for an ailing sister, she was terribly excited.

"Why ever is it taking so long, do you think?"

The hostess, a pert young woman in a plum-colored garrison cap and uniform, promptly adopted the soothing tone applicable to scheduling fumbles: "They're attaching a private car down from Alaska, ma'am. Going down to Palm Beach for the winter." She rested a knee on the empty seat beside the teacher and leaned low to see out the window.

"My, that must be someone very important," the schoolteacher said.

"There, look." The hostess pointed at the platform. "Ever heard of Klondike Callie Fisk?"

The teacher put her hand up to cover her mouth, as if her excitement might lead to excess. "Oohhh, is that the one they made that musical about?"

"There she is."

"She's still alive? She looks wonderful. Who are those two handsome men with her?"

The hostess, glib by profession, hesitated. "Well, ma'am, actually, those are her husbands."

"Husbands!"

The hostess sounded a little wistful. “I guess that was a time when you could be anything you wanted, if you had the nerve.”

“My goodness.”

About the Author

James David Buchanan grew up in Birmingham, Michigan. He attended Michigan State University where he obtained a degree in something he had never studied. He also attended The New School of Social Research, California State University-Northridge where he studied Criminology, and UCLA, studying Irish literature. Buchanan was active in the Civil Rights movement, and has worked as a jazz musician, in a brokerage office, as a stage hand, television director, Hollywood studio tour guide, casting director, schoolteacher, television producer, screenwriter, and novelist. He has had five novels published, four of them in Great Britain and three in German, French, and Italian. His next **Five Star Western** will be *Welcome, Suckers*, the title of which is derived from the masthead of the Creede, Colorado newspaper: **PLENTY OF SILVER, PLENTY OF GREED, WELCOME, SUCKERS, TO THE CITY OF CREEDE**.